PRAISE FOR

THE RUN FANTASTIC

"Witty, absurd, and utterly enjoyable. Luke Kondor is the future of Bizarro fiction." —Carlton Mellick III, author of *Satan Burger* and *Sweet Story*

"Equal parts hilarious, moving, and very, very weird. The entire Bizarro genre's been put on notice—Luke Kondor is one to watch!" —Brian Asman, author of *I'm Not Even Supposed to Be Here Today*

"A dark fable full of emotional heft and humor. Luke Kondor comes at you sideways, surprising you with universal truths beneath a whacked-out Bizarro veneer. *The Run Fantastic* is constantly entertaining, and right up my alley." —Danger Slater, author of *I Will Rot Without You*

"*The Run Fantastic* is the funniest meditation on death I've ever read." —Amy Vaughn, author of *Skull Nuggets*

"I'm very impressed with Luke's brain. I think he should send *The Run Fantastic* to David Firth so he can make an animation to accompany a reading of this entire book, that's how unsettling, hilarious and Northern *The Run Fantastic* is. It's full of clever metaphors, daft as a *Mighty Boosh* episode and so beautiful in places that everything about humanity, love and death makes sense, if only for a minute." —Madeleine Swann, author of *Fortune Box*

"*The Run Fantastic* is some poppin', lockin', crackin', clickety-clackin' stuff. Get on it, son!" —Douglas Hackle, author of *Terror Mannequin*

"Damn, this book has heart. And guts. And mangled flesh. And dead things and flying things and metaphors that will make your ears pop and dialogue that will light up your funny bone. And I HEART that the main character is named Ampersand (see the set-up here?). AND is the word that keeps on going. And. And. And. Left. Right. Left. Run. Fan-f&&&ing fantastic." —Charles Austin Muir, author of *Slippery When Metastasized* and *This Is a Horror Book*

THE RUN FANTASTIC

LUKE KONDOR

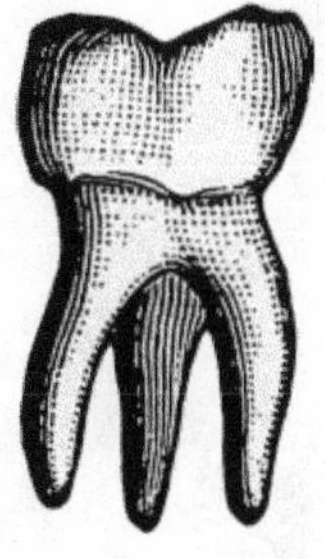

ISBN: 978-1-950305-71-1 (sc)
ISBN: 978-1-950305-72-8 (ebook)

First printing edition: August 27, 2021
Published by Bizarro Pulp Press in the United States of America.
Cover Design by Nicholas Day | Layout by Don Noble
Proofreading and Interior Layout by Scarlett R. Algee
Edited by Nicholas Day

Bizarro Pulp Press, an imprint of JournalStone Publishing
3052 Sassafras Trail
Carbondale, Illinois 62901

Bizarro Pulp Press may be ordered through booksellers or by contacting:
JournalStone | www.journalstone.com

THE RUN FANTASTIC

PART ONE

"To die will be an awfully big adventure."
— J.M. Barrie, *Peter Pan*

1.

HAVE YOU EVER noticed that everybody is called Ross these days? Apart from the ones that aren't, I mean. Everybody else. Nine times out of ten. They're a Ross.

Ampersand Jones used to be a Ross.

His name had been Ross Jones for his entire life, right up until his twenty-first birthday when he got the call from his parents explaining that they had changed their minds.

"We just think Ampersand suits you better," is what his mother said.

"What do you mean, mum? It's too late for all that. My name is Ross. You can't change your mind now!"

"We didn't *want* to change our minds, Ross... Sorry, I mean, Ampersand. The world just turns on its own, y'know? Sometimes you find yourself in a place you never thought you would be. And we found ourselves in a place where we'd given you the wrong name. We're very sorry, Ampersand, but that's just the way it is."

"I can't believe I'm hearing this... Is dad there? Can you put him on?"

"One second," she lowered the phone, called out to his father. "Ross!?" His father was *also* a Ross.

The phone switched hands.

"Uhm... hello? Is that Ampersand?"

"No... it's me."

"...Ampersand?"

"My *name* is Ross."

His dad sounded like he was nodding.

"Dad, can't you speak to her? I can't be changing my name at twenty-one. Think of all the paperwork."

"Well, no... don't worry about all of that, son. Mum's taken care of everything. You should be getting your new passport through the post any day now... I think the driving license will be two weeks. Of course, you will have to change all of your bank account details. She's worked very hard to change your name, Ross... uhm... Ampersand, I think you could show a bit of appreciation, don't you?"

"But my name is Ross!"

"No, son. *My* name is Ross."

2.

ROSS... *AMPERSAND'S* MOTHER was right. The world does keep turning; it shifts beneath you with or without your permission and sometimes you find yourselves in unexpected places, in peculiar situations. And sometimes, you *don't* find yourself at all. You fall through tectonic cracks in time and space, forever asking yourself the question: Just who the hell *am* I?

Ampersand couldn't help but feel like his feet were never where they should be; he often found himself unmoored, the world spinning beneath his heels, faster and faster, ready to push him off and leave him adrift in the sea of space, floating away, forever coming to terms with himself and his lack-of-place in the universe.

It wasn't long after he became Ampersand that he met his wife, Dottie. She had a birthmark on her face and wore braces and smelled of talcum powder and she liked to wear yellow skirts with polka dots. She told him how she used to have a fascination with ampersands and that she would draw them all over her school books in permanent marker.

"On their sides, they look like infinity," she said.

"Yeah, I guess you're right. Or racetracks," Ampersand said.

She explained that she didn't stop drawing them for years and she wasn't sure why...

"But now it makes sense," she said, before leaning in for what would be their first kiss of many.

3.

THE WORLD TURNED a little more and Ampersand and Dottie fell in love. They moved in with each other and then consequently moved out together. They left university and went to London, had to take out a small loan in the process, hoping to experience life in a big city while they were still young, something they couldn't say for much longer.

Unrelenting, the world kept turning and after only a couple of years, they moved back to the countryside, ready to escape the hustle and bustle and smog of city-living. Dottie had suggested they save up to buy a house of their own and get a dog and purchase a car on a finance deal and also, she wanted to eat out in fancy restaurants more. Ampersand simply nodded along.

What else could he do but bear it and smile? As much as he may have wanted it to, the world refused to slow down. Things kept changing, more so with every passing moment. With the power of bank loans and credit cards, they got married at twenty-five and went on a two-week honeymoon in Mallorca. All-expenses paid.

At twenty-six, his hair thinned and his metabolism slowed. At twenty-six and three-quarters, he had a bald spot on the back of his head and where he'd been a slim man for most of his life, he'd put on nearly two stone of pure fat. He had to buy new trousers and shirts on store credit. He even signed up to the local gym and bought special shoes purely for exercise. He went to the gym *once*, got scared off by the amount of hard grunting, and spent several hours hiding in the Jacuzzi. He never went back and also never got around to using his special shoes. They remained in the box, gathering dust at the bottom of his wardrobe.

And with the student loans, council tax, and stacking loan repayments, he was forced to get a *proper* job in an office and was forced to contribute to a pension and to his chagrin... open a savings account.

Ampersand didn't want the world to keep turning.

He very much wanted it to stop.
Or at the least, slow down a little...
I just need a moment to catch my breath, is all.
Please!
Just a moment!
For fuck's sake... a moment!!!

4.

"I'M PREGNANT."

They were twenty-nine years old when Dottie came out of the bathroom, holding a pregnancy test, smiling like she'd won the lottery, cheeks beetroot red.

"What?"

Her words snatched the air from his mouth, left him gasping.

"...we're going to have a baby..."

5.

AMPERSAND CRIED AS he hugged her, kissed her, lifted her shirt and kissed her stomach repeatedly, giggling and snorting, saying "I can't believe it."

"Stop!" Dottie bellowed, exploding with giggles and snorts. But he didn't. Never before had he felt such elation at any single piece of news. His body fired up with adrenaline and he jumped with joy, fist-pumped the air. He called his parents and they joined him in his excitement, told him to make sure to pick the right name, and then he called his sisters and his aunties and his uncles and then his granddad and then he went to social media and posted on Facebook and Twitter and Instagram.

GUESS WHO'S GOING TO BE A DADDY!

And Dottie did the same, telling family and friends over long emotion-heavy phone-calls, tears and smiles and pleasant worries.

Together, they celebrated, wanting the moment to never end, already a little sad because they knew, like all moments, that it would.

6.

"THIS IS IT," he told her as they drank their tea that night, readying themselves for bed. "This is where life starts. I'm going to work three times as hard at the office. I'm going to open a *second* savings account… sure, I'll have to pay off my student loans first but so be it. And I'm going to start drinking green tea… and I'm going to download some self-improvement podcasts. I'm really going to *live,* y'know? And… and… and I'm going to run a fucking marathon!"

Dottie chuckled.

"A marathon?"

"Yes… why?"

"I've never seen you run before."

"So?"

"It's just really far, is all."

"How far?"

"Twenty-six miles."

"Really? That is *actually* quite far, isn't it?"

"Yes."

"Still… I'm going to do it for our child. I'll run a marathon. Sure. I'll do anything. In fact… I'll do it tomorrow. I'll get up tomorrow morning. I'll get up even before the sun. What time is sunrise?"

She shrugged. "Erm… six-ish."

"Fucking six!?" He nearly dropped his cup of tea. "That *is* early. Still… I'll do it. Tomorrow morning. I'll set my alarm now. And I will get up, and I'll go for a run."

Dottie just smiled at him, a little bewildered at his wild claims. He could see the doubt in her eyes but he was on top of the world and he was certain that this was *it.* This was where life began.

"Well, okay then," she said.

"Well, okay."

Buzzing with the possibilities of what may be ahead of them, they finished their tea. He cleaned up the mugs and put them away, his heart still rattling around in his chest, too excited to sit still.

Beneath his feet, he felt it.

The movement of the planet.

That moment to catch his breath would have to wait.

This is it, he thought. *This is it!*

As Dottie climbed into bed, asleep before she even finished yawning, Ampersand set aside a pair of shorts and a t-shirt. He dug out a headband from the sock drawer. It was a gift, a joke, on account of how unlikely it was that he'd ever use it.

Who's laughing now, eh?

He snickered, remembering the time he claimed that he was allergic to exercise, that it brought him out in fevers and made his skin blotchy. Still, here he was, setting a headband aside and completely prepared to use it.

He took out the shoebox from the bottom of the wardrobe, blew the dust from it, and opened it for the first time. The special running shoes he'd bought all those years ago, finally ready to be put into use.

The new-shoe smell filled the room as he took in how bright the yellow fabric was, how clean the red laces were, how springy the flappy middle bit was.

They were perfect.

The adrenaline was leaving him by that point, making space for the exhaustion to fill. He was quite sure that it had simultaneously been the shortest and longest day of his life. Setting his phone down on the bedside table, he climbed into bed, and looked upon his sleeping wife and thought about how this was *it.*

This...

This is where life begins.

He clicked off the bedside lamp and quickly, and deeply, drifted into sleep.

And then promptly died.

7.

WELL... AMPERSAND WAS never *a prompt* person. What would take a normal man mere minutes took Ampersand several hours to do. It began with a blood vessel in his brain, somewhere between the cerebellum and medulla, bulging at first, before popping open like a ruptured cyst, blood running like rivers through the folds of his brain, slowly filling his skull with dreams of red. This was at 3 am. By 4 am, he was crying scarlet tears, his brain now drowning, his fingers gently shaking. By 4:45 am, his heart had slowed to a dangerously slow beat, his skin turning alabaster white, some heavy bruising around his eyes and neck and his joints. By 5 am, Ampersand Jones was completely and utterly deceased.

But still... the world kept turning.

At 5:45 am, the alarm on his phone rang out. It was loud, grating enough to wake a dead man. And that it did. Groaning, Ampersand reached over and turned it off. Without a second thought, he climbed out of bed and put on the clothes he'd set aside the night before. He put in his headphones, running the cable beneath his t-shirt and into his shorts pocket.

He slipped on his headband, checking himself in the mirror as he did, paying no mind to the dried blood on his nose or in his ears or how his eyes looked like exotic fermented eggs or that his lips looked like garden slugs. He simply readjusted his headband and winked at himself.

Finally, he kissed his sleeping Dottie gently on the head, leaving a bloodied oval stamp. He kissed her a second time, thought how the two kiss-imprints looked a little like an ampersand... or a racetrack... or infinity.

"Wish me luck," he whispered, to his unborn baby, to his wife, to his family.

By 6 am, Ampersand Jones, cold and dead, headed out the front door and went for a run.

PART TWO

DEATH WARMED UP

"...in this world nothing can be said to be certain, except death and taxes."
— Benjamin Franklin

8.

IT WAS A blue morning. Quiet. There was no birdsong, only the slightest breeze, and the sounds of Ampersand's shoes metronomically hitting the concrete. Each step echoed through the empty streets of Keyton – the town that he and Dottie had called home for the best part of three years.

Ampersand ran to the end of his cul-de-sac, past the closed gates of the primary school, all the way to the high street, past bakeries and corner shops and florists with their shutters down, past closed bars with abandoned pint glasses with the last of the night's beer sitting on the walls out front, past the supermarket, normally buzzing with life, people driving to and from, filling up on petrol and shopping, all peaceful now, quiet.

He couldn't remember *ever* being awake before 7 am. Had he ever seen a sunrise? He wasn't so sure. This was a different time and therefore a different world, everything resting in its gloom, waiting for the day to click into place.

He continued to run, focusing mainly on his feet.

Left. Right. Left. Right.

It was pretty easy stuff.

He didn't focus too much on *where* he was going, only on the dashed white lines on the road, guiding him onwards like pale fingers *come-hithering*.

Well this is nice, he mused, to be alone with his thoughts, to be awake before anybody else, to live in a world all of his own, a place where everything was silent and still and there were no new bills or office politics or health concerns or noises in his car promising future breakdowns.

And he was running. He was *actually* running. Something that he had told himself he would do for years and was finally doing it.

He was pumping hard, lifting his knees up to his middle and slamming his feet down, pounding the concrete with each step, running like a loosed prisoner, free at last.

Why didn't I try this before?

Perhaps running had been his calling in life and he'd never known it? Some were born to paint, others to write, some to inspire crowds with their oration, some to choke people out in the Octagon, some to sell used cars, some to make software and games from blank documents and text, and perhaps Ampersand was born to run. Perhaps he would end up as a world-famous runner — the first guy to circumnavigate the globe by foot. Imagine that! Or the first person to run to the North Pole. Or the first person to run to the moon. Yes. This was it! He was going to change the world one step at a time.

His smile widened, all teeth on display, greeting his morning with all the gratitude he could muster.

But where *will you run to,* he thought, scanning the roads leading in and out of the town, wondering which route would be the least affected by traffic. He didn't want to worry about being run down by cars or trucks or cyclists. And he didn't want to worry about getting lost. And he didn't want anybody to see him; he couldn't stand the idea of being caught trying to improve himself.

He needed somewhere straight; he needed somewhere desolate.

9.

JOGGING PAST THE abandoned police station, he rounded the corner to see that nestled between the police station garages and the corner shop was a gap.

It was about three-feet wide, and definitely wasn't there the last time Ampersand looked. Through it, he saw road and little else. It was dead, more so than the blue morning, more so than a cloudless sky, void of sun or moon, more so than his Grandma Sue at the open casket funeral, looking the same but empty, like the soul had been scooped out through the eyeballs and the lids sealed shut. She was gone, sure. It seemed her body was only waiting to catch up.

This gap seemed much the same, something dead that didn't quite know it. As if someone had reached into the world and scooped out a hole, made the perfect place to run undisturbed, to escape the coming noise of the world, the judging eyes and expecting hands, always asking, always needing.

Look, man, the gap seemed to say. *Isn't this exactly what you asked for?*

Ampersand walk-ran to the opening, leaned his hands against the pebble-dashed walls. He felt cold fingertips rake the lower of his back; the pool of blood in his brain pulsed. Unease prickled his throat.

"Seems perfect," he said. With a deep breath he took the six small steps required to pass from one side to the other. Without looking back, he ran on, passing a sign that said YOU'RE NOW LEAVING KEYTON.

He ran through an archway of trees that reached over the road like steepled fingers, tightening its grip the further he went in. There was darkness at the end of the tunnel and only when he came out the other side did he find a cool brightness that burned his eyes.

Squinting, he looked at the concrete road as it came into focus; it was everlasting, bordered by hills and grey grass, empty gloom-filled fields ending where the trees took over; tree-lines that stood up at the edges of his vision like inky brushstrokes splitting ground from sky. He left the pavements and smooth tarmac and all that was familiar behind him and was now running on the side of the road, the road that didn't turn or curve or rise or fall, simply went on, into *whatever lay beyond.*

10.

STILL THINKING THAT he was purpose-built for forward motion, Ampersand continued that same quick pace for all of a minute before he started to slow. The chill wind picked up and sweat pearled on his forehead. Heat buzzed through his chest and arms, needles prickling in his fingertips.

Already? he thought. *How can I be getting tired already?*

He was breathing harder now, each laboured breath grating against the insides of his lungs, sounded like he was sawing wood. Even his steps were coming out of sync.

Left. Right. Left. Left.

No.

Wrong!

Right. Left. Right. Right.

Double-right!?

What the fuck are you doing!?

As his steps lost their rhythm, so too did his breathing.

Out. Out. In. Out. In. In. Out. Through a single nostril. Then two. *In through the ears!?*

No!

Wrong.

Wrong!

WRONG!

Running like a glitching computer game character, arms flapping out at the sides instead of back and forth, legs now stepping forward at the same time, he realized what he was doing could no longer be classed as running, instead a repeating standing jump.

At least there's not much further to go, he thought to himself. *I must be about done, right?*

He slowed, reached into his pocket and pulled out his phone. He had downloaded a special running app that tracked the distance, monitored his pulse, and to play his inspirational running podcasts.

First, his eyes went to the phone signal. Zero bars. And then to the distance meter.

"What!? How is that possible?" he said. "Half a mile!? But that's..." He walked to the side of the road, planted his hand against a tree. He ran the numbers in his head. It took him a moment. "Twenty-five and half miles left!? That can't be right."

Wiping the pink sweat from his cheeks, he thought that perhaps he should turn back, maybe he should give it all up. If he played it right, he could be home before Dottie woke up, could be there with toast and coffee ready. She would be so pleased that she'd forget all about his run and his utter failure. She'd say thanks and tell him how wonderful he was.

But she would know. Wouldn't she? Maybe she wouldn't say anything but she would know deep-down, in her middle, right where the baby's growing. All those shame-thoughts curdling like old milk, souring the amniotic fluids, right in the fucking womb. That baby is going to hate you. And for good reason. You're the fool who thought his calling in life was running all of three minutes ago. Now look at you. You can't even get the order of legs right. It's left right left right, dumbass. How difficult is that? And you breathe in through the nostrils and then out through the mouth. Simple.

"It's more difficult than it looks," he said, lied.

I can't believe you ever thought that you were the kind of person who could make their life better...

He wiped more red tears from his cheeks, thought about Dottie, his baby, his pride. He sucked in several huge breaths before setting off again, slower this time. He pressed the play button on his phone and slotted it back into his shorts pocket.

Ampersand took one last look behind him at Keyton, saw the glowing amber sunlight rising behind. Already, it looked impossibly far away and would only get further away from here on.

I just need a moment to catch my breath, he thought, thinking about the world, its unrelenting expectations and pressures, crushing him flat under its thumb, mashing him into the concrete.

"I'll be back," he whispered, lied, before turning away from them — his family, his town, his world. "I just need to catch my breath."

Ampersand ran along the empty country road, heading away from the sunrise and chased the darkness.

He settled himself in for a long day, week, life...

And then the inspirational podcast began to play.

11.

THE PODCAST OPENED with music, swelling choirs, angelic, the kind that made you think you were being lifted into heaven in a column of light. Then there were drums. A simple loop. Some strings. Orchestral. Probably a royalty-free song snatched from the Internet.

The music was followed by a voice. It was deep and close and had the timbre of a man recording from *inside* the microphone, gave the impression that you didn't have a little headphone in your ear but a full-sized man, naked with his knees tucked up, his warm breath tickling your ear drum, sweaty hands playing your cochlea hairs like a harp.

The man spoke:

"Hello and welcome to another episode of 'The Really Inspiring Running Podcast' with me... your host, Chris Tangle. Goddammit, I hope you're ready for this episode, because it will change your life!

"On the last episode we talked about the importance of a good stretching routine, about how we need to look after our muscles and our joints and our ligaments and how we do that by spending some quality time before and after our runs pulling them apart until they hurt real good. Nice! We want to build relationships with our muscles, deep and personal. I want you to fall in love with your legs. *I* love your legs... you should too.

"We also agreed that the best way to run is the way that I tell them. We agreed that the people who run like I tell them turn out to be the best runners. Didn't we agree with that?

"Yes.

"Yes, we did.

"So today... it may not make sense to the majority of you listening right now but this episode isn't for everyone. How best to explain this but... I have been working with a life-coach. I know, I know. Even *I* need a life-coach every now and again. This guy, he told me to dial down my target audience... that I should know *exactly* who

I'm talking to. And like everything I do, I've taken this philosophy to the MAX! I've dialed my target audience down to one.

"Are you listening right now? I'm sure that you are. I bet you're out for a run right now, aren't you?

"Yes. That's right. My audience of one. You're out running and you're alone and the sun has only just risen. Am I right?

"You can talk back, y'know? I can't hear you, but that doesn't mean we can't have a conversation.

...

...

"Well?"

Ampersand was slightly confused by this point, but at least the confusion took his mind off the burning sensation in his thighs.

"Ampersand. Are you listening or what?"

For a second there, Ampersand thought the podcast host said his name.

"Listen, Ampersand, if you're not going to talk this whole podcast is going to be a little one-sided."

"Are you... are you talking to me?"

"There he is! The little runner!"

"Wait... can you hear me?"

"Nope."

"But it's like you're talking to me."

"Yes."

"How?"

"Who knows how the world works, Sandy. I can call you that, right? Good. The world is a mysterious beast and its secrets are hidden deep. I can't explain air. Can you?"

"Erm... I think it's just different molecules or something... they're light enough to float and we breathe them in and the oxygen is absorbed into the capillaries in our lungs and–"

"–No! ...you *can't* explain air. Or batteries. Or space. Or Wi-Fi. And don't even tell me you understand why people like jazz!"

"I... you got me there."

"Exactly. We don't know *how* it works, Sandy. But it still does."

"My name isn't Sandy."

"I know that. *Whoa!* Look out for that stick!"

Ampersand stepped over a lone stick, lying in the middle of the road.

"How did you know that a stick was there?"

"I didn't."

"Right."

"Like how I don't know that your wife is pregnant... like how I don't know that you're constantly plagued by fear of bankruptcy or paying back your student loans... like how I don't know that you're dead."

"I'm not scared of student loans!"

"Sure you are."

...

...

"Did you say I was dead?"

"I'm afraid so, Sandy. Check your heart monitor."

"What heart monitor?"

"On your phone."

"Right."

He lifted it from his pocket.

"Swipe right."

"Hang on a sec."

He swiped right and there was the heart monitor. Where it would normally give a sharp up-and-down, mountains with red peaks and green bottoms, there was only a flat line.

"Oh yeah... I see what you mean. Bloody hell. I don't remember dying, though."

"No, I don't remember you dying either. But look at you! You're dead and you're out for a run. That's really quite inspirational."

"But I've got so much left to give."

Ampersand wiped a bubble of bloody snot from the end of his nose. He sniffled, whimpered.

"Hey... come on, Sandy. Don't beat yourself up. Who knows... maybe if you run hard enough, you'll come back to life? Maybe if you run a marathon, the gods will make an exception."

"What gods?"

"I dunno... like... Zeus and that."

"Would that work?"

"Who knows? What I will say is... did you ever hear about the guy who ran the *first* marathon?"

"Uhm... Usain Bolt?"

"No... this was a *long* time ago, Sandy. The first guy to run a marathon was a Greek man, a messenger. He ran twenty-six miles from a place called Marathon to another place called Athens to announce that a war had been won. Don't ask me which war.

Anyway… he ran *really* hard and *really* fast and after he delivered his message, he straight up died."

"Straight up?"

"Straight up."

"Shit."

"Shit, indeed. My point is, Sandy, that perhaps if you were to run a full marathon, being dead and all, it might have the reverse effect. If it made a living man a dead man, why can't it do the opposite and make a dead man a living man?"

Ampersand's brain bubbled. He found out he was dead just a moment ago and then he found out that maybe he could reverse the death by running a marathon a moment after that. It was a lot to take in in less than a couple of moments. His brain bubbled some more.

"…interesting," he said finally.

"I mean it's just math, right? You can't argue with the math."

"You're right, Chris." Ampersand took in a deep breath, in through the nostrils out through the mouth. He gritted his teeth and picked up the pace. "I can *not* argue with the math."

12.

THE GREY-BLUES of the skies had melted away and left only a hazy amber. There wasn't a cloud in the sky and oddly, there wasn't any sun either, just a thick sheet of honey-soaked cotton wrapping the world.

On either side of the road there were crumbling and uncared for dry-stone walls, sectioning off patchwork fields of green, peppered with red poppies and unmoving sheep, white and quite dead, fixed to the ground like desiccated clouds.

The white lines on the road had faded to near nothing, worn away by time and feet. It was fine, though. Ampersand didn't need to follow the white lines anymore. There were no forks in this road, no sudden turns, no decisions, only forwards.

"Careful now, Sandy. You've got to pace yourself. Watch that heart rate. Oh yes. I forgot. You don't have a heart rate. Never mind about that... but the pace, Sandy. Watch the pace! Good good. That's the ticket. I think you've really mastered the basics of running. There's not much else to it really. Now you just need to do the same thing for another twenty-three-point-eight miles. You got this."

"But my feet are hurting."

"Remember, Sandy. Ninety percent of running is in your head... and the other ten percent... is in your mind."

"That doesn't make sense."

"You're overthinking it!"

"I am?"

"Get your head out of the game!"

"But you just said it was all in my head."

"Forget about what I *just* said... and think about what I'm going to say next."

"Which is?"

"...I don't know. I haven't thought of it yet."

Just as Ampersand was coming to learn that there was a surprising amount of mental arithmetic involved in running and maybe motivational podcasts weren't all they were cracked up to be, a woman passed by on the left. It was so sudden that he nearly missed her, her feet gunning, arms pumping, dressed in form-fitting running gear, royal blue and aerodynamic, whistling as she cut through the air.

By the time Ampersand caught sight, she was already a little way in front, casually turning her head, ponytail swaying. Ampersand couldn't quite make out the finer details of her face but he could see that it was too white, looked bleached, her eyes too wide and her smile too huge, the corners pulled unnaturally high.

Numerous medals bouncing around her neck, clinking, her running form perfect, a gazelle that dreamed it was human.

"Nice day for a run," she called out, teeth never parting.

"Morning," Ampersand tried to say but it came out as an explosive cough. He sawed the spit from his chin with the back of his arm, hoped she didn't notice.

"You see anyone around here?" she said, glaring light reflecting off her bone-white forehead.

Ampersand tried to speak again, mustered up a soft wheeze, managed to shake his head.

"That's too bad." Her eyes were on him and through the burning light he saw that she had no eyelids... no face, in fact. "Try lifting your knees a little more," she said. "It'll take the strain off your back."

He tried to say thanks, but it was too late for that. The faceless woman was already far ahead, disappearing into the deepening hole of the horizon like a particle of light tumbling into a black hole.

"Wowzers," Chris Tangle said in his earpiece. "She was hot stuff, am I right?"

"You saw her?"

"No, Sandy. I'm not there with you, remember? You're really taking your time to get to grips with this, aren't you? I can see my kitchen table where I record my podcasts and I can see my USB microphone that I got from Amazon and I can see my sports drink. I can't see anything else."

Ampersand tried to lift his knees a little, tried to pull his shoulders back, mimic some of the blue-runner's form.

"But she *was*, though, right?"

"I have a wife. I don't notice things like that."

"Sure... and that's why you're running, is it? Because you love your wife?"

"Yes, of course. And my unborn child. Why? Why else would it be?"

"No no... I got you. It's all above board."

"That's right."

"Okay."

"Okay."

13.

"MAN, I'M FUCKING hungry. This has been the longest podcast I've ever recorded. Normally these things are done in like twenty-minutes. I jump on, record some inspirational chit-chat and then I'm done. A bubble bath and a dirty magazine and then it's time for bed. If this thing goes on any longer, I might just get the magazine out here and now treat myself to a bit of *me*-time."

"Please don't."

"I can't promise you that, Sandy. Now keep those knees up. Focus on your form, your breathing, and the road. Can you do that? You keep that form and I'll keep the magazine in the drawer.

"*Lusty Long Legs.* There's some inspiration for you! That's my favourite magazine, by the way. *Lusty Long Legs.* Wow... you should see the calves on some of these girls. And men. I ain't picky. It's all about the legs for me. Did I tell you that I loved legs?"

"Yes."

"Good, because I do. It's like I always used to say... to my legs.... just this morning, in fact, I said 'I love you, legs. I really bloody love you.' If I had to pick my favourite part of a leg, I would have to say I'm partial to a calf muscle. There's something about the upside-down heart shape of the calf that's like a hot-blood injection right into my—"

Ampersand removed the headphone from his ear, let it dangle down by his side. He could hear Chris's tinny protests undulating, shouting to be heard, but Ampersand wasn't listening anymore. He was too busy looking at the dead creature in the middle of the road.

It was naught but a tawny rag, filthy and twisted with bloodied ends. There was a tire track running through its middle, crushing it deep into the concrete.

He hated the thought of some poor creature choosing to cross the road at the wrong time, left to bake in the summer days. He could relate to the dead critter. He, too, had felt crushed by things outside of his control and he, too, was dead.

As he passed it, keeping a wide berth because it smelled and looked gross as shit, he tried to make sense of what it was but couldn't make head from tail, foot from claw, couldn't even see where the road ended and the critter began.

He tried to forget about it, tried to focus on the task at hand—running. But it wasn't long before he came across the next dead animal in the middle of the road. This one didn't have fur but ochre-coloured feathers speckled with gold and pink. It had most of its head, but little else.

And then Ampersand passed another, and then another, and another. Crushed squirrels and burst house cats, rolled fox kits and a headless puppy. Flies buzzed around each of them, disturbed as Ampersand's feet shook the road beneath them. There was a sour-rot smell hanging on the air, reminded him of music festival toilets and vinegar and the butchers where his dad used to take him.

"And where do you think you're bloody going, chap?"

The voice was quiet at first, papery thin, was most likely in his mind but he turned his head anyway, looked over his shoulder to see faces. There were only a couple at first, but then they all looked up, peeling their heads from the road and looking at him. Eyes reflecting the amber skies back at him, all of them looking like somebody had but disturbed their nap time, not their deaths.

"Are you listening or what?" said the voice again, and this time Ampersand saw that it was coming from the badger carcass. Its head was crushed. Brains like strawberry ice cream pushed through the crack in the top of its head. "Or are you of the ignorant sort?"

Ampersand had stopped now, was looking at the assemblage of roadkill unsticking themselves awkwardly from the floor, dragging themselves towards him.

"I'm... I'm listening but... who are you?"

"My name's Gary."

"I'm Susan."

"Anthony."

"Craig."

"Kenny."

"I'm Ben."

"Nelly."

"Ross."

They were coming from the edges of the road now—the ones that hadn't died right away but hadn't made it much further, return of the living roadkill.

"Are you going to eat me?" Ampersand said.

The gathering dead looked at each other, offended, scoffing at first before chuckling.

"I don't think so, pal. I haven't eaten anything for days now and I don't plan on changing that now," said the fox with the missing eyes, maggots dripping out. "Because I'm dead."

"Dead things don't eat," squeaked a squirrel from down by Ampersand's feet. He took a step back.

"And they don't run around neither," said the badger.

"That's a double negative, Gary," said the pheasant.

"Yes, I know. It's *very* negative." The badger tried to pat its brains back into his crushed skull, failed. "You can't be running around like that... being dead and everything. You'll make us look bad."

"But I have to run. I have to run myself back to life. I need to run a marathon and then go and see my wife and our baby. I've got stuff to do, y'know?"

They laughed as if Ampersand had said a funny joke, but stopped when they saw that he was serious. The roadkill looked at one another, their whispering chatter like fingers through tall grass. Carefully, they looked up again.

"No, we don't think so, chap," said the badger. "No offence, but we don't believe that you deserve all of that. Otherwise, you wouldn't be dead in the first place. Dead people don't die for no reason."

"Double negative."

"Very negative."

"Yes."

"Super negative."

"Bad juju!"

"Dead people don't die for no reason!" said the badger again, louder, his voice crackling like a bag of broken glass.

"I know that! There's been a mistake. I'm not supposed to be dead! Now I have to run and fix it. I *have* to."

A sudden pain flared in Ampersand's shin. He looked down to see the dead squirrel. Its yellow-cracked teeth were sticking into his leg. It unstuck them and then called Ampersand a "Cunt".

"I beg your pardon!"

More offended by the word than the bite, he kicked the squirrel over the side of the road into a bush. Now the other roadkill was coming towards him, grumbling and wheezing.

"I'm sorry, pal," said the fox, "but we can't have you moving about like that, upsetting the nature of things and our feelings of self-pity."

"Who gave you the option to go and improve your life like that!?"

"Not on our watch!"

"You'll have to stay dead like the rest of us. Stay broken!"

The burst cat shrieked as it tried to jump at Ampersand, but it got caught in its own intestines and tripped, crashing face-first into the road. Ampersand quickly booted it like a football down the road trailing a fluttering line of pink rope. The badger with the brains was surprisingly quick, though, and his mouth looked strong and he had all his teeth. He gnashed at the air, billowing out mouthfuls of dust with each bite, loosening more of his brain with each snap. Ampersand jumped back a step, tripping over the head of the pheasant, hitting his backside on the ground.

"Prick!" said the pheasant-head.

Ampersand got back on his feet within seconds, turned and ran up the road, limping a little, but still much, *much* faster than the growing horde of broken-bodied critters who were now behind him, still peeling their mashed bodies from the floor.

"You better run!" one of them shouted. "No wait... don't!"

But Ampersand was already running.

"Don't worry."

"He won't make it far."

"He's a giver-upper if ever I seen one."

"Too fat... too lazy..."

"He ain't a runner."

"He'll hit the wall..."

"He ain't never gonna run a marathon."

The headless dog howled through the hole where its throat once was.

Ampersand was running again, terrified by the creatures he was leaving behind, not of what they would do to him, but of ever becoming one himself, of collapsing into his skin, giving up on maybes and somedays and accepting the truth of it all.

You will never escape death.

The voice came unbidden, was his own, echoing from somewhere deep down in the roots of his brainstem, in the gluey puddle of blood that had set there. He didn't want it, though, and quickly thumbed the headphone back into his ear, wanting to disappear into his inspirational podcast–

"Oh yes... you sexy thigh... oh so... so close... I'm going to... nearly!"

–and then he removed it.

Instead, Ampersand just focused on the sound of his breathing and getting to the end of the road. Though it didn't matter how far he ran, the end only seemed to be getting further and further away.

14.

LONG-DISTANCE RUNNING didn't sit well with Ampersand's short attention span. His legs couldn't quite keep up with his wandering mind. At one point, he felt the road dip, and then a little more, declining deeper and deeper, descending into a down-ramp, no longer leading to the horizon but into a hole in the ground.

As he ran deep into the earth, the darkness and the moist smell of soil cloyed at him. All around he heard his loved ones; they were saying their goodbyes; his throat burned with all the words he would never be able to say.

"He was a good son... our Ampersand," his mother would say. "I only wish that he could have done more pull-ups."

She was right. Ampersand had never been able to do a pull-up, and it was something that had plagued him since he was a teenager. What would he do if he ever found himself hanging over the side of a cliff, or off of a bridge, or found himself in a situation where everybody at work was doing a pull-up competition? What the fuck would happen then!? Everybody would find out how weak he was, he would just die... he would *just* die.

"I loved my husband," Dottie would say, probably wearing a black veil and black blouse and that same favourite yellow skirt with the polka dots. "But he made noises in his sleep... and he never finished painting that shed in the garden. So, I'm glad he's gone, really."

I'm sorry, he wanted to shout. *I ran out of paint... I have sleep apnea. SLEEP APNEA!!!*

The consonants were trapped in his esophagus, the vowels caught in his teeth.

Ampersand went deeper, saw worms on either side of him. They were the size of busses, eating and shitting dirt, eating and shitting dead things.

He heard another voice. Unfamiliar, and yet he knew exactly who it was.

“I never knew my daddy,” the boy or girl said, tears boiling out. “I wish he wasn’t so selfish and didn’t go and die before I got to meet him.”

Ampersand wiped the scarlet build-up of tears from his eyes as he disappeared deeper into the darkness. The coffin was up ahead. It opened up for him. It was lined with white taffeta. It looked comfortable, cozy even, welcoming him with an endless hug.

He closed his eyes and ran into it, expecting to feel the cushions against his face, to hear the snapping shut of the door behind him as the casket swallowed him, but there was nothing. There was only the running and the road, the running and the road, the running and the road, the running and the road, the running and the fucking never-ending road...

He opened his eyes and he was back... above ground.

There was no more darkness; no more crying loved ones; no more worms, only that same hazy amber sky.

And a car.

15.

THE CAR ROLLED at a leisurely pace. It was the size of an ant at first, growing bigger. It pierced the air with an electric whine as if the motor was a beehive, popping erratically as though rolling over unseen light bulbs.

Where there should have been joints and gaps in its body, it was smoothed over. The dark glass rolled over the top half in one smooth piece like a bubble of tar. The rest of the car was the colour of mint ice cream, spattered with dead flies and dirt. The wheels were caked in bits of animal and mud and the back-left tire was almost completely flat, bulging at the bottom like the belly of a fat man who'd unclasped his belt.

Ampersand had never seen a car like this, but up close he recognized that it was a self-driving car. One of the fancy ones from Las Vegas or Los Angeles or wherever. One that came with a free kale smoothie and probably a coupon for a floatation tank. It was the kind of car that you program the destination in and sit back and let it do the driving for you. On the roof, there was a large marble rolling in a cradle, a crystal ball from which an all-seeing eye could peek, a camera lens, spinning, blinking, observing. Every few moments, the lens winked and with a slight jerking motion, the car righted itself, making sure to stay dead center of the road, robotically avoiding potholes and other hazards.

The camera watched Ampersand as he neared it, uncannily following his movements. Its iris dilated as it focused on him, before looking away, back to scanning the road.

Coming up to the side of it, Ampersand tried to peer inside the driver's side window but the tinted glass was too dark to see through. A chill rolled down his spine, told him that there was someone on the other side of the window, looking back. In the reflection, he saw himself... and he waved.

Nobody waved back.

His skin suddenly felt too small for his bones.

Running faster now, aiming to leave the strange robotic car behind, he heard the winding down of the car window and from the open gap poured the stink of rot and spores and decay floating outwards like sand caught on a breeze. It was the smell of excavation and exhumation, digging up something long since buried. You could say… it was like opening the tomb of Tuten-*Car*-mun…

…

Ampersand snickered at the author's joke, but stopped when he heard the voice from within.

16.

"WHY BOTHER?" THE voice from the car said. It was the voice of an Indian man who'd spent a year gargling pennies.

Ampersand slowed, peered inside the window and saw utter shadow. A face pushed forward, surfacing from the gloom, revealed itself, the cooked-egg-whites of the eyes and the crooked smoke-stained teeth; Ampersand could just make out where the decomposing body had become enmeshed with the fabric interior of the car, stitching flesh and polyester, car and man.

"Why bother what?"

"You can't escape, my friend. No escape. Even in death. The tax man always comes." With each word spoken, more of the rot-stink spilled out and Ampersand's gag-reflex shuddered.

"Not that it's anything to you," Ampersand said, nettled. "But I'm running because I need to get back to my family. I've got a baby on the way!"

"Well, you're running the wrong way, is what I'm saying."

"My podcast told me that this is the correct way to run. So... y'know... who should I be listening to? The running podcast guy or the dead guy in a self-driving car?"

"Fair play... fair play... I'm just saying... why have abs, y'know? I prefer kebabs. Why *run* when you can have *fun*? Why exercise when you can just... I don't know... *not* exercise. That's my philosophy, my friend. Let everything else do the work."

Ampersand's eyebrow twitched.

"I've got a machine at my house that not only toasts my bread but butters it, too. I've got a gadget that wakes me up in the morning and percolates my coffee. You don't have to do stuff yourself anymore... we live in a world of outsourcing. Stop running.... Climb inside.... let the car do the moving for you."

Ampersand didn't say anything.

"Seriously. Come join me. It's nice in here. I have AC."

Still silent.

The dead man sighed; the smell was fucking awful.

"I'm only saying because... no offence, but you don't look much of a runner."

Ampersand's cheeks grew warm.

"Look... mate... sorry... but who the hell do you think you are? You can't be talking to me like this. You don't know me. For all you know I could be the world's greatest runner."

Ampersand's foot slipped on a pebble. He quickly righted himself.

The man chuckled; the car whined and popped.

"I know exactly who you are, my friend. I know because we are the same. Deep down. You might as well climb in and take a ride. There's plenty of space in here with me. You won't get anywhere faster, but you'll still get there. Know what I mean?"

"I don't know what you mean." Ampersand kept his eyes ahead but continued to listen, imagined climbing into the wheeled crypt, hand slipping in unseen corpse-bits, boiling up between fingertips, getting lungful of dead man's dust. "No way, José," he said.

"My name is Ravvy. Not *José*."

Neither of them spoke for a moment. There was only the wind, the breathing, the footsteps, and the whirring motor. The car dropped behind but quickly caught up, bringing Ravvy's smiling shadow back in line with Ampersand.

"What!?" he shouted.

"Seriously... get in. You can meet my friend. She's resting up, been running a long time, y'see. We're having a fucking nap party in here... sleeping and remembering the good times, good food, good TV. I miss them all now. Don't you?"

Another sudden jerking motion and the car avoided a rock.

"You know who I don't miss? My girlfriend! I love her and everything but I just can't bear it. All those expectations are like one of those anvils that crushed those cartoon characters. You know the kind I mean?"

"Sure. The coyote guy..."

"Yes... the coyote guy. The big ACME fuckers that landed on him. I feel like I got one of those above me and I'm in its shadow, just waiting for it to land and crush me into a pancake. Man, I miss cartoons. You know I had this TV... you should've seen it... flattest TV you ever seen, and from the side... you *couldn't!* Thinner than a slice of paper. *And* it used to record all my favourite shows. I'd just clock in the kinds of things I like to watch and it did the rest for me. *Stranger Things... Daredevil... RuPaul's Drag Race...* Technology's great man. You should try it."

Frustration rose in Ampersand's chest in a bubble, readying to pop. Still running, he turned, said, "Why are you talking to me?"

The man in the car laughed, each chuckle spitting out more spores of mould and decay. "Ah yeah, yeah... I had a point. So, my girlfriend. We've been together for years now. How long? Who knows!? I've lost count. I was going to break up with her. We had a good run but sometimes you know it's not right... y'know?

"I should have done it years ago, but I was scared. I was scared of hurting her feelings. I was scared of being alone. I was scared of having the conversation. I'm *still* scared, my friend. I'm terrified. But I got in the car and set in the coordinates to her house... because I knew that it didn't matter how scared I was. I had to do it. I *had* to... and I set the car to take me... no matter what!" Ravvy's voice snapped, came out like a distant scream.

Ampersand picked up the pace but the car lurched forward, bringing him in line again. There was no escaping the man's spiel. The car wouldn't allow it.

"But on the way to break up with her... I got all sweaty and out of breath and then I felt these shooting pains in my left arm, and then the faintness took me, and then the pains weren't just in my arm but my heart. My fucking heart, man! I shit my pants, friend. I had a heart attack and I shit my pants... right here in this car... but even still, I was sort of grateful... because it meant that I didn't have to go through with the breakup. Thank the heavens. I'd gotten out of it... or so I thought. That was a while ago now. And look... we're still talking and the car is still driving."

"Good for you, then," Ampersand said through gritted teeth. "At least you escaped the thing you didn't want to do."

"No, my friend. You don't understand. I died... sure... but nobody can escape. Not really. The coordinates are set. The car will still take me to her, to face my duty, whether I want to or not. Like I said, my friend. We are the same. The tax man is coming for both of us. There's no escaping our responsibilities."

"The tax man?"

"Sure. Why not? Everybody owes something. It's just about whether we're ready to pay or not. Why do you ask? You miss a repayment?"

Ampersand didn't answer.

"Shit. You did!? Student loans? Yeah that'll get you. You gotta pay the bill at some point. Me? I wonder how long my girlfriend has been waiting. Man, is she gonna be pissed when I finally arrive."

Ampersand was pulling ahead now, unable to slow down, finally leaving the self-driving car behind. He was running faster, faster, his eyes swelling, wanting to cry but no tears came. He closed them, trapped it all inside. The pressure in his head grew. His skull was readying to split down the middle, crack open like a Venus flytrap.

Behind him he heard Ravvy shouting: "You really should just get in... come and meet my friend... maybe she can help you run better!"

Ampersand ran and Ravvy began to sing tunelessly about the tax man, about how he was '*cometh*'. His voice dampened as the car window rolled up, and the car fell behind.

Ampersand was breathing harder now, pounding his feet so loud and so fast that he didn't notice that the fields bordering the road were becoming barren; the green and the blues of the skies were now gone, replaced by dying ochres and burning yellows, the rolling grassy hills becoming desolate, the horizon starting to shiver.

17.

A Quick Tune from the Whistling Man

THE TUNE BEGINS with a low hum, an up and down melody that you might mistake for the breeze, billowing through the loose leaves and detritus of the road, bristling through the dirty hairs of the road kill, wending its way to Ampersand's spine, bringing chills and concern and making people say, "Somebody just walked on my grave."

But that's further on down the road...

It begins like all things... at the start. The old man who smells of sweets and shit and dry piss laces up his running shoes, pulls up his socks, ties the band of his shorts, and takes his first step. He starts with his good leg, and then the bad one. At the same time, he purses his lips and begins to whistle. Here the wind picks up and the loose gravel rolls and somebody somewhere starts to wonder what happens after they die.

"It's like... the big question," says a guy in California with dreadlocks and a doobie.

"I think it's where we reconnect with all of our loved ones," says the daughter of a preacher over a boiled-egg and grapefruit breakfast.

"I hope there's bacon," says an Englishman, drinking bad coffee and talking to no-one in particular. "Bacon and poontang."

All of them are neither right nor wrong nor are they real. I made them up. The only thing they need to know is that at some point... the Whistling Man will find them.

He goes by many names, by the way, does the Whistling Man. Some call him the Limp Father, because of those millions of lives he took before they were born, now nothing but semen stains on the ends of his running shorts, the ones who were never named. Some call him the Tax Man, because of his never-ending pockets, full of receipts, unpaid bills, and accounts of unpaid student loans. In those black holes, he carries an up-to-date financial record of everybody who decides to run on *his* road, and by all accounts — *all* roads are his.

Some call him the Rag 'n' Bone man, gathering the unwanted bits of trash and loose ends, making damn well sure they're forgotten about as promptly as possible. Some call him Father Time, some call him Kronos, and some call him the first great idiot, a man who loses days like a gambler wasting coins on the slot machines. And some call him History, because of his function (not so much his intention), to roll you up in the road, bury you in ever-deepening layers of events, under pages of crushing details and memories and names. If the old man has anything to say about it, the world will forget about you, and the quicker the better.

He's a slow runner and he knows that, but he is of the tortoise-persuasion (and he has the leathery skin to prove it). He is slow but unstoppable, the first moving force of the world, the one who put the bodies into motion in the first place.

Some might just call him a happy man.

After all, he is the one who whistles while he works.

PART THREE

HUMAN HEAT

"Life is pleasant.
Death is peaceful.
It's the transition that's troublesome."
— Isaac Asimov

18.

"YOU HAVE JUST passed the six-mile mark. That is really fantastic work! Especially for somebody so slow and lazy and fat. I'm surprised you made it this far, to be honest. You're unbelievable! How do you feel?"

Ampersand couldn't answer; he could barely breathe. His body felt like it was breaking down, his gums tasting like furniture polish, his legs no longer his own, replaced with feather pillows stitched on with single threads. His back throbbed, felt like an anarchist had moved into one of his kidneys and set the walls on fire. "Fuck the Man and everything he stands for!"

His eyes, too, were rebelling against him, seemed to be working their way out of his skull like botfly larvae, stretching eyelids, tearing and *maggoting* their way to freedom.

"Visualize your goals, Sandy. Picture yourself as somebody successful, perhaps a little less around the waistline. Maybe picture yourself driving a sports car. Picture yourself naked, racing a bull, and winning! Picture yourself like you're a giant turtle made of diamonds and imagine you're best friends with Patrick Stewart. He's trying to call you but you're too busy right now... being a fucking turtle! That's right: *you're* too busy for Patrick Stewart. Is that too far-fetched? Sure, okay.

"Try this one: know your *why*. That's a good one. Erm. Be the man you want to be... not the man you are. No? Okay how about, you only fail if you stop. What about... you don't have to be great to start, but you have to start to be great?"

Ampersand made a noise like a deflating balloon and Chris clicked his tongue.

"I've got to be honest, Sandy, I'm pretty much out of inspirational *bon mots* here. How about I jump on Google real quick and dig us up some more inspirational slogans? One grunt for yes... two grunts for no..."

Ampersand deflated some more.

"Okay, wait right here... and by here, I mean remain in motion. I'll fire up the laptop, and will be back quick sharp to get you all inspired again. Okay?"

Ampersand wheezed.

"Great. Back in a jiffy."

It didn't matter how many inspirational sayings Chris Tangle fired at him, Ampersand knew that there was only so much gas in the tank and the warning light was flashing, the engine lurching, the machine rolling with momentum and little else.

Rest, then. A power nap. A bath. Maybe a glass of milk. Or a banana. Imagine that!? A fucking banana!

Whatever. He needed something and he needed it fast. He was exhaustion now and nothing else. Just hot air wrapped in cling film, marker-penned up to look like a man, deflating and floating to the floor. Also, his nipples were chafing, were hot and itchy and he was fairly sure something was bleeding, just wasn't sure what.

He wanted to quit. He was a fool to think he could ever run such a distance without any previous training. Even back in school, he'd find a way to duck out of P.E. He'd complain that he was sick, or that his allergies were playing up, or that his toenails were too long.

So why start now? he wondered. *Why start running the day after you find out about the baby? Think about it...*

Why are you running?

Better yet: what are you running from?

Chris Tangle said to "know your why". So maybe think about it for a second. What's your why – why run, why breathe, why do anything?

Ampersand didn't have an answer. He imagined that it wasn't him that was asking the question but his unborn baby, a handsome little fetus, open-water eyes and toothless curiosity, at the crossroads of chromosomes. He pictured himself telling his child about his aversion to exercise, about how he'd lie to his parents and tell them that he was on the school football team and how he was a key part to their recent victory. He scored the goals, Mum. He kicked the ball into the net better than everybody else, Dad.

He pictured lifting his son or daughter up as they fiddled with their umbilical cord. They barely weighed anything, were meringue light. Sitting their blue-grease fragile butts on his knee, he confessed that he once hid in the bathroom for three hours because he didn't want to play in the school football game.

The imaginary baby erupted with disapproving tears and Ampersand confided that he never scored a goal, didn't even understand the *offside* rule. More explosive tears and wails and his fingers sank into the baby's putty-flesh.

"I just hid in the toilet stall and I cried," he said, the baby's eyes sinking into its face, the legs dropping from the body, slapping the floor, his hands meeting in the middle. "And I played Pokémon on my Gameboy. *Pokémon*!"

No baby anymore but gunk and shame and he was left to wonder how he could be an example for anybody. How could he tell a child to aim for better if he never did himself? He couldn't even stop his baby from melting...

Why are you running, daddy?

The puddle of baby shuddered.

Why?

"Why anything?" he said. "Why *anything!?*"

19.

AMPERSAND'S LEGS WERE moving slower and slower, his feet sinking into the concrete, shoes growing heavier, knee-joints clicking like knots in fire.

"Listen, Sandy." Chris sighed into his ear. "I've given you just about every inspirational slogan in the book and you're still running too slow. I don't think they're working. I mean... look at you... it's like you're stuck in slow-motion, like you're a buffering video. And did I mention, you have twenty miles left to run!? Twenty!!! You've given it all and you've only ran six miles. Not bad, I guess, but do you think you've got another twenty miles in you? Because, honestly. Speaking as your inspirational running coach... you *can't* do this."

Chris's words were ten-pound weights on Ampersand's ankles.

"It's okay," Chris continued. "You gave it your best shot and you did well. So, what if you are just too much of a failure to continue? Tons of people are failures. You don't see them trying to run themselves back to life, do you? *Do* you? I'm genuinely asking. I can't see, remember?"

Ampersand shook his head; a string of saliva hung from his chin.

"I didn't think so. Listen... I'm speaking not only as a coach but as a friend. We've known each other for about an hour and a half now. I think we're pretty close, right? So, nothing left on the table here... from friend to friend... I think you should give up."

Ampersand's feet stopped moving, seemingly by Chris's command. His chin dropped to his chest; his eyelids closed. The breeze on his back was cold, swayed him on the spot.

"You've let yourself down, Sandy. Your wife will wake up tomorrow and you won't be there because you'll be dead, and she'll know because of the bloodstains on the pillow, and deep down, she will understand it's because of how rubbish you were... but mostly, more than anyone in the world, you know who you've let down?

"*Me*, Sandy. You've let *me* down. I had such high hopes for you... such high hopes..."

Ampersand pictured Dottie waking up to the empty space next to her. She would know, wouldn't she? It would be written in the empty space in the bed, in the creases in the bed-cover, spelling it out: *Ampersand Jones is a massive fuck-off failure.*

He opened his eyes and looked once more to the horizon. He saw now that the earth on either side of the road was scorched, the trees bare, brittle like pigeon bones. The grass had given way to rolling waves of sand. The skies were turning the colour of orange peel, and although there was the constant breeze blowing behind him (a breeze that scared the dying life out of him), the air was growing sticky, hot.

He removed the headband, used it to mop the sweat from his brow, cheeks, and mouth, before putting it back on.

Why are you running?

"Because I'm scared," he said to nobody, wasn't sure where the words came from but made about as much sense as words could. "I'm fucking terrified," he said again, huffing in a deep breath.

Well, at least you can admit it...

Well done...

Now move...

Slowly and steadily, Ampersand started to move again, gradually building up to his running pace. He nodded to himself, took the win, however small it was, and continued on.

I'm still scared, he thought.

And still, you run...

"It worked. I knew it! You thought I was a bastard just then, didn't you? Well I just Googled reverse psychology and looks like it did the trick. Actually, that was some great coaching I did there. God I'm fantastic at this coaching! Oh yeah, nice work to you, too, Sandy. Keep going and all that."

Somewhere in Ampersand's mind, the baby still cried and something was still bleeding, but he was running again... and that was enough for now.

"And don't worry," Chris continued. "If you ever feel like stopping again... I'll be there to make you feel like shit. I promise."

20.

A quick aside...

BACK AT THE house (Number 23, Downside Drive, if you were interested), Dottie's usually twitching eyes were still. In her dreams, she saw nothing, felt nothing, was absent. The town of Keyton remained trapped, locked in the blue world, holding its breath, the gap next to the police station scabbing over like a cut across a fingertip, wanting to heal, to bury old pains in new flesh, to shut forever.

Somewhere else, a man was running.

21.

AMPERSAND RAN TOWARDS the dizzying heat-haze on the horizon and through the waves of reality he saw people, runners, *lots* of them. They were only a small handful at the rear but a clenched fist at the front. Their procession was the length of two busses, all of them matching each other's pace, legs pattering the floor in unruly syncopation, kicking up small clouds of dust in their wake, their running shoes all the colours of the neon-rainbow, sweatbands and knee-supports, all wearing a uniform blood-red t-shirt.

Their footsteps grew louder as Ampersand neared. The ground recoiled with each step. So loud then, he could barely hear the sound of his podcast, now but a whimper amongst the shouting feet.

"Now *these* are runners!" Chris Tangle yelled so loud his microphone distorted. "These folks know how to move their legs and breathe air! Take notes, fatty! I mean, Sandy! Now this is the stuff! This is what running looks like! Not that I can see anything mind you. But... you know what I mean!"

Ampersand caught up with the one at the back. That was a mistake. The runner was a laugher, already chuckling to himself before Ampersand arrived, more so after making eye contact. Ampersand nodded a hello. That was a second mistake. This was a ruddy-cheeked man with white tennis socks reaching up just below his knees, teeth like a hamster, looked like a clay figurine not left long enough in the kiln, features not quite set.

"Ha! Hello! Hahaha! Nice day for a run, wouldn't you say? Glorious, init? Heh!"

The man couldn't say a word without a quick burst of laughter, his cheeks quickly turning the colour of a boiled lobster, of a toddler who'd banged its head and only just realised, of a sunburnt father who'd fallen asleep by the pool, an inflamed lymph node, chip-shop greasy, hot to the touch.

"HAHAHAH!"

“Excuse... me... sor... ry... do... sor... ry...”

Ampersand tried to speak but couldn’t get a word out between gasping breaths.

“Looks like you could—ha!—do with a pick-me-up. Here take this!” The man lifted his t-shirt, revealing a pouch tied around his waist. He unzipped it and pulled out a shiny silver packet that said LIFE+ on the packaging. Tearing off the end of the packet with his teeth, the tomato-faced man handed it to Ampersand. His fingers were slick with sweat and Ampersand nearly dropped it but he clutched it tight, pulled it to his mouth and sucked hard. A burst of sour fruit-flavoured cream filled his mouth, shooting down the back of his throat and flying down into his gut. It had the colour and consistency of pus, pulpy with strings that caught on his tongue, lassoed his tonsils.

For a moment Ampersand held his hand over his mouth, forced himself to keep it all in. Once settled, he licked his fingertips, sucked as much out of the foil wrapper that he could before handing it back to the man, who simply threw it to the side of the road where it landed by an upturned ribcage. The skull connected to it lifted up, made hollow eye contact with Ampersand, then looked at the runners, shrugged, before lying back down.

22.

"THAT'S SOME NOS-grade energy gel, chap, haha. Shouldn't take long before you feel a wave of fresh running fuel burning through your veins. Heh! Oh, and you may need this?"

The man reached his clammy pink hand into the pouch once more, pulled out a clear plastic bottle of water. He handed it to Ampersand and wiped his hands against his shirt. "Go on," he said, nodding. "Drink it."

"I'd do as he says, Sandy!" Chris Tangle was still shouting to be heard. "Unless you brought your own gels and water! Did you?"

Ampersand shook his head.

"Didn't think so."

Ampersand shot a quick squirt into his mouth before handing it back, already kicking himself for not drinking more. The man blasted some into his mouth and then over his forehead before placing it back and zipping his pouch up. He was calming now, introducing himself with *almost* a straight face. "I'm Plip Betcha!"

"Tell him about me," said Chris Tangle. "Tell him about my podcast."

Ampersand ignored the crackling shouts in his ear, was too busy feeling the wave of fresh energy roll over him, the energy gel rushing his bloodstream. Suddenly, his joints weren't straining quite as much and his straight-backed posture was returning. The sandpaper dryness of his throat now mostly gone.

"The red shirts?" Ampersand said with a cough. "Are you a club?"

"Ah yes... hehe... for better or worse, these teammates of mine are stuck with me... ha! I'm the slowest one. And as the Red Engines say, you should never leave a runner behind... which means that I bring the pace of the whole club down."

"You're not slow," Ampersand said. "You're just steady."

"That's mighty kind of you to say, sir! Hehe!"

"I've never heard the name Plip before."

"It's short for Phillip."

"Isn't Phil short for Phillip?

"Yes... but Plip is even shorter! Ha!"

"Is it?"

"What's a name anyway? Plip. Phil. Nobody cares about a person as an individual! Am I right!?"

"No, I guess not."

"It's the bigger machine that matters... not the cogs! Hehe. That's not to say that the cogs don't need a little grease here and there."

Plip pointed to the wall of runners on the right and said, "We got some Stevens, Alex's, a couple of Louie's, a Ronald, a Matthew, a handful of Bertie's." He pointed to the left wall. "And over here you'll see Noels and Rajeshs and plenty of Muhammads and Mustaphas and a smattering of Daves."

"You got any Rosses?" Ampersand said.

"Oh yes," Plip nodded enthusiastically. "Can't move without bumping into a Ross here."

"No girls?"

"No no! Ha. Certainly not! This is a men's running club. Our captain always says that women are distractions from the running and that we must abstain from stationary delights."

Plip placed a hand on Ampersand's shoulder. When the man guffawed, his whole body shook, the laughter travelling like an electrical current through Plip's arm and into Ampersand. His body quivered as the chuckle rattled around in Ampersand's gut, before fluttering up through his throat and escaping out through his mouth like a dove from a magic hat, escaping in the form of a titter.

"*Heh.*"

Plip pulled Ampersand closer, still running (always running). His breath was minty, the gap in his front teeth widening. "You've got a good sense of humour. We like that in the Red Engine Running Society. Are you affiliated with a club yourself?"

Ampersand shook his head, not just at the question but at being so close to Plip's mouth. The man looked like he could swallow him whole.

"No."

"Fantastic! Hahaha! This is a match made in heaven then. We only but yesterday lost one of our numbers and are looking to replenish our troops."

"I don't know if I want to join a club. I'm only running today—"

"—Nonsense! Running is a lifestyle! Plus, it's for a good cause! Ha! It's up to runners like you and the Red Engines to keep the planet moving. If we were ever to stop, well the whole planet would come to a halt, and there would be no more days, no more hours, no more minutes. People would freeze on the spot, spoons of tomato soup would never reach mouths, planes would never come into land, suicide jumpers would never hit the ground, and an apple would never land on Mr. Isaac Newton's noggin. Hahaha! Imagine a world like that. A world without gravity!"

Ampersand tried to but was immediately stopped.

"No don't! That's exactly the kind of world we *don't* want. Time has *got* to pass by, buddy. Things *have* to go on... even if sometimes we don't want them to. Heh. We run because we're good people. We run because we want to save the world. Ha! Do you agree?"

Ampersand didn't know what to say.

"I don't think you have a choice here, Sandy. Considering that these guys have energy gels and water and you have such an unhealthy lifestyle... this is your only shot at running the marathon. My advice as an inspirational running podcast host is to use these guys for all they've got and then ditch them when you finish the marathon."

Ampersand swallowed, said, "Okay."

"Bloody brilliant!" Plip slapped Ampersand on the back, nearly bowled him over. "I knew you'd join the cause! Come on you've got to meet the others!"

Plip grabbed Ampersand by the hand and yanked him forward, pulling him deep into the moving bodies of red, stopping briefly at a wall of runners. There seemed to be more of them now, more the deeper they went. They were running close to one another, some linking arms, stitching themselves together. They were so tightly woven that it seemed impossible to pass through but Plip tapped one of them on the shoulder and two of the runners unlinked their arms and stepped aside, opening up a gap... or a doorway.

With a quick turn, Plip winked before pulling Ampersand inside.

Suddenly, engulfed in sweat-stink and hot-breath and pulsing arms and throbbing veins and pumping insecurities, Ampersand realized how small he was compared to the other runners. They were all so tall, seemed to be getting taller the deeper he went.

Ampersand couldn't see above their heads, couldn't see the world beyond the engine, and couldn't stop or slow down as the wall of runners behind him pushed him onwards, backwards, bumping him deeper inside.

Some looked over at Ampersand but most didn't seem to notice he was there. Too lost, they were, in agony of movement. Their faces were hot pink, skin dusty with the dried salt from their own sweat. Some nodded to Ampersand with hell-faces, others eyed him but went back to focusing on their running, huffing in deep breaths and pushing it out through gritted teeth, spit flying forth and landing on their chins.

Some look okay, Ampersand thought, but the deeper into the running club he went, the more he realized that that wasn't the case. Many of them had blueish bruised skin, dark bags around their eyes, some with bandages around their heads instead of sweatbands, some with deep gouges in their arms. Some missing limbs altogether. Some with missing eyes, toothless mouths in their place. Some with intestines tied around their bellies instead of belts. Some with ragged holes in their heads, missing throats, slit wrists, exposed bones, missing jaws...

Oh, Ampersand realized. *They're all dead...*

Plip continued on, his grip on Ampersand's hand only tightening. He took him around more walls of bodies, tapping on shoulders and opening more doors, closing others behind him, unlinking runners' arms and linking others, rearranging, sealing the engine shut, pulling Ampersand deeper and deeper into the labyrinthine corridors of exhausted and dead bodies, still running, running, running.

Ampersand was barely able to keep up the pace, even stepping on a couple of the runners' shoes.

"Hey fuckface! Watch it!"

"Move it, fatty!"

"Cock."

Ampersand waved his apologies and went deeper still, the air growing unbearably hot, both from the yellow skies above and from being in the heart of a perpetual human-powered engine.

The sweat-stink pressed heavily against Ampersand's chest, squeezed his lungs tight like an office worker's hands on a pair of stress balls, rinsing the oxygen out of them like water from wet flannels.

How many bodies deep was he now, he wondered, unsure if he could break through the walls and escape even if he tried.

“You know I’m not too sure about this anymore!” Chris shouted, voice breaking up. “I liked it better when we weren’t completely surrounded.”

Ampersand would have agreed but was suddenly yanked again by Plip, pulled to the far wall, to the line of men facing forwards.

“Teddy!” Plip shouted, letting go of Ampersand’s hand and cupping his mouth, shouting at what appeared to be a giant. “Oi! Teddy! We have a new soldier in the fight against No-Time! Haha! He’s a real card, let me tell you!”

Without missing a step, the one called Teddy turned. Head first, then body, then legs. Now running backwards, he was looking down at Ampersand like a dish best served running. Some of the others making up the walls were curious, too, and were turning to see the new recruit. All of them were running backwards, sideways, forwards, perfectly in sync. It was a super-organism, and Ampersand was caught in its middle, about to speak to the brain — the one they called Teddy.

Also, Teddy had three legs.

23.

"SO, YOU WANNA run for the greater good. Yes? If not... that's cool. I don't give a fuck."

Teddy's voice was foghorn loud. It cut through the din like torchlight in a dark cave. The constant running appeared to have no effect on his speech at all, didn't hitch or falter with each step or breath. If Ampersand couldn't see his legs pounding away like pistons, right, middle, left, he wouldn't have thought the man was running at all.

"Haha, yes... he most certainly does! Ha!" Plip said, hand still on Ampersand's shoulder, keeping him from slowing down or turning away.

"And what makes this one think he's good enough to join the Red Engine Running Society? But, like, even if he was good enough... I wouldn't give a fuck."

Teddy had one of those beards that people who can't grow beards have. It looked like kindling, like a strong wind might blow it away. If the beard was supposed to hide his broken face, it was failing... hard. It didn't hide his broken nose, which was angled slightly to the right, or the sunken right eye. Nor did it hide the gashes on his neck, or the torn earlobe. Something terrible had happened to the man's face and no amount of facial hair could hide it.

"It's fine," Ampersand shouted. "I really wasn't set on the idea anyway—"

"This isn't some sort of weekend running club for the half-hearted!" Teddy trampled through Ampersand's protests.

"Honestly... I'd be happy to leave right now, if you could maybe show me the way out, I'll be on my way—"

"Fine! We'll give you a shot, fat-man! We'll give anybody a shot to prove themselves to the Red Engine! After we lost Keepsy to those mermaids yesterday, we could do with an extra pair of hands. Or better yet... feet. I don't give a fuck. But prove to us that you have what it takes or we'll go ahead and throw you overboard, see if I give a fuck. I'm warning you now... I won't."

There was a cheer and a laugh from the others.

"Overboard?" Ampersand said. "But we're not at sea."

Teddy scratched at his beard.

"That's what they all say," he said. "Right before we throw them overboard."

24.

"I DON'T KNOW if Plip told you, fat-man, but if we were ever to stop our running, the planet would stop rotating. What do you think to that?"

"He very much doesn't want it to happen. Heh!" said Plip.

"That's right. You *don't* want it to happen. Movement is our god, running our saviour, and we pray twenty-four hours a day with our feet. You understand? Not that I give a fuck."

"Oh, haha, he definitely does!"

"Good good."

In his earphone, Chris Tangle wouldn't stop talking about Teddy's third leg. It was just as defined and functional as the regular two, wearing exactly the same sock and shoe, wearing a special pair of shorts made for a three-legged man. "The guys got legs for days," Chris kept saying. "Legs for days!"

"We can offer you free gym membership at your local sports center." Teddy continued, "A discount card for all your energy gel requirements, and protection from exhaustion from the dangers out there on the road. With our support, love, and performance enhancing supplements, you will never *not* run again. Tell me, fat-man... are you in?"

"I don't... I don't..." Ampersand's eyes were now on the many medals hanging from Teddy's neck. There was gold, silver, bronze, swaying left and right, left and right. He looked to the other Red Engine faces, gurning and running, pained, caught in perpetual-motion hell, unable to stop for fear of realizing they'd put their faith in the wrong thing.

How could a person cope with that, Ampersand thought to himself? *To come to terms with the fact that they'd made the wrong choice?*

Plip gave him a short nudge on the shoulder.

"How do you know?" Ampersand said.

"I beg your pardon?"

"How do you know that the world would stop turning?"

Teddy burst into laughter. Plip was already laughing. The others joined in.

"Oh, right. Yeah, we don't *know,*" said Teddy. "We don't *know* anything. Who could really *know* a thing? But this isn't about knowing... this is about trust. We have to trust that we don't know and know that we have to trust.

"Let me tell you, Plip only started running because he wanted to lose a couple of pounds. Next thing you know he's running every weekend and at lunchtimes, going on special running holidays. And then he's signing up for a running club, he goes for a few longer runs and then one day he wakes up and is like... woah... this isn't just my hobby but my religion. *This...* I give a fuck about *this!* I'm unstoppable! *We're* unstoppable! Running isn't something you set out to do. One day you wake up and realize you're *already* running. By then, it's too late. So, join us... and be unstoppable, too. Or don't. Like I said... I really don't give a fuck."

"Well... this is it, Sandy," Chris said. "This is who you are now. You're a runner. Better just accept it and become another bit of wall or whatever. At least you'll run the marathon... but then you'll just keep running more and more of them... keep on running forever I guess... running and running and running and running and running and running and running and running and run—

25.

TEDDY REACHED INTO his pouch and pulled out a red shirt, unfolded it, and handed it to Plip. The shirt wasn't new, wasn't clean, was patchy with old bloodstains.

"This t-shirt belonged to one of our best! Ha!" said Plip, moving towards him, holding the t-shirt up as if planning to suffocate him with it.

"Wear it... and prove to the Engine and to *yourself* that you can do this," said Teddy. "Or don't."

"But I only wanted to run a marathon. I don't want to save the world!"

Teddy wasn't listening now. Red hands reached out from the walls to help Plip push the shirt over Ampersand's head. Claustrophobia and the stink of someone else's blood, sweat, and tears, caused him to gag. He panicked as the many arms pushed it over his neck, threading his head through, were about to push it down over his shoulders when they stopped suddenly, their hands falling away.

In one motion, the running club turned and looked to the skies. Somewhere, someone was playing a bugle horn.

The horn played again, a brass toot from the front of the engine. The grand 'shirting' of Ampersand was halted. A second later and there was another flurry of bugling before a distant voice called out: "In the skies!"

"Upwards!"

"Gulls!"

Somebody screamed.

26.

WITH THE T-SHIRT still around his neck, Ampersand followed the runners' eye-line to see three silhouettes swooping in circles above, fluttering amongst the glare, zipping and spiraling, a downwards corkscrew aimed at the runners. The skies dilated; the silhouettes swelled; the glare burned his eyes; he thought they weren't gulls but...

"Angels?" he asked the skies.

It didn't respond.

Instead, Chris did. "Don't think so, Sandy. Just massive fucking birds."

The birds' bodies were sleek and their wingspans huge. Ampersand was transfixed by the graceful way in which they flew, barely noticing as their silhouettes grew bigger as they dived towards them, wings pinning back.

They grew to the size of beach balls, diving then swooping, diving then swooping, passing over the Red Engine's heads, watching with baited breaths.

Ampersand could see that they were people-sized white birds with dirty feathers and searching eyes, cawing madly with each pass. He was mesmerized, didn't understand how a bird could get so big.

The first of the great white bastards swept across and the runners ducked. The second swept past Ampersand's unsuspecting face and he saw it in all its glory, its imperfect feathers, pupils not quite true dark, a drop of milk in black coffee. He could smell the salt on its breath, feel the sea-breeze brush against his sweaty forehead. Its dirty claws were long. They snagged the face of one of the runners as it passed over, but didn't find purchase. It hooked the shoulders of another, snatched the runner upwards.

"On guard!" Teddy called out as the third and final gull swept through, coming towards him. "Or don't!" Quickly, he reached into his pouch and pulled out what looked like a small knife.

Brandishing it like it was a full-length sword, he jumped upwards, his three legs powerfully launching him towards the gull. They seemed to freeze in mid-air for a moment, the gull's beak inches from Teddy's face and his knife inches from the gull's throat. Ampersand saw Teddy's mouth moving, already knew what he was saying. There were tears, though, running down Teddy's eyes. Ampersand wondered if he actually *did* give a fuck. He wondered if maybe Teddy gave a whole load of fucks.

Time clicked back into place and Teddy and the gull tangled and dropped from the skies, landing in the gathering of runners, catching both of them.

A moment later, and the walls separated and in came Teddy, bloodied knife in teeth, a twitching gull in his arms like a baby fevered with nightmares. Runners cheered and Ampersand couldn't stop himself from joining in, but stopped when the distant cawing sound above pierced the fanfare.

Up above, the other two gulls stole away with their prize, the runner struggling for his last time.

They watched in horror as the two gulls wrestled the red runner between them, pulling him to pieces bit by bit, catching most of the dropped pieces, missing some, which rained down a little ways off the road, organs hitting the scorched floor like blood-red water balloons.

27.

THERE WAS SILENCE as the Engine passed the gull carcass between them, plucking feathers in turn. When it came to Plip, he ripped out a handful from the gull's tail and threw them up into the air. With a lump in his throat, he shouted: "This one is for you, Ralph!"

Ralph, presumably, was the runner whose innards were spread up and down the roadside like jam on toast.

The feathers drifted upwards, caught by the wind, before settling on the road behind them. Plip's laughter had mostly gone, but he still couldn't hold down the occasional titter, and nobody was sure what he was laughing at but they didn't mind it at all.

When the gull was passed to Ampersand, he tried to avoid its staring eye. It was the size of a grapefruit, prehistoric, dead but still looking. Ampersand looked at his own reflection in its pupil and maybe the pupil dilated, maybe it didn't. Dead things had a habit of living on this road. Still, he felt an incredible wave of guilt wash over him when he plucked a single feather from its shoulder and threw it into the air before passing the gull further along.

"Ralph was a good man," Plip said, wiping his eyes. "He'd fought the good fight with us for a long time now but he was young, raw... could've made for a captain one day. Heh!"

"Captain? You mean like a boat captain?"

"Oh, yes. Well... the Engine *is* like a boat in many ways. The hull itself is made of runners. And we occasionally have to scrub the deck. Ha... but that's because we have a guy called Dec and he stinks like shit. Isn't that right, Dec?"

A somber voice from somewhere in the wall: "Aye."

Ampersand absently checked his phone, saw the same flat line where his pulse should be, saw that the podcast was still playing, and that he had now passed the twelve-mile mark. That meant he'd run another six miles and had barely noticed it. Either the energy gel or the excitement had done the trick, and though a note of happiness buzzed through his system (*I've run twelve miles!*), it was quickly followed by Chris Tangle reminding him that he was only just coming to the halfway point.

"Don't worry though," Chris told him. "You're never going to stop running now. These boys here will see to that. Oh, yes... you're just another cog in the machine now, Sandy, and it seems these boys will run themselves into oblivion or infinity, whichever comes first. You may as well get used to this, Sandy. This is what you are now. This and nothing else."

He ignored Chris, didn't want to think about forever just yet.

"How did you come to this road, Plip?"

Plip wiped his mouth and took another swig from his tiny bottle of water before handing it to Ampersand, who drank much deeper this time. He hacked it back up as the liquid burned his tonsils, spitting it over his front.

"What the fuck!?"

"Moonshine. Made by some of the boys on the left flank. They've got fermenting system in place, running copper tubes through their sleeves. The secret ingredient is sweat."

"It's not very secret if you tell everyone."

"No, not secret... *secrete*... as in, the ingredient that they *secrete* from their glands and that. Was that not clear?"

"Fucking Christ."

"Yep. For me... it was never so much about running or losing weight or anything. Heh... as you might be able to tell. In fact, before finding Teddy, I don't think I'd done much exercise at all in my life. Put it this way... I was the guy you put in goal. I was big enough to get in the way of a ball without having to run for it. That was if anybody wanted me to play in the first place. Ha. I didn't have too many friends."

Up ahead, at the front of the Engine, Ampersand saw the gull carcass raised up. Its body was now completely featherless, testicular pink. The runners parted to let Teddy run over and inspect it.

"I read a blog post that said running was a great way to meet people," Plip continued. "And it is... I just didn't meet anybody until *afterwards.*"

"After what?"

Plip looked at Ampersand as if sizing him up, deciding something. Another chuckle fell from his mouth like loose chewing gum. He turned over his right arm, pulled the wristband down and over his hand, and Ampersand understood.

There were several pink lines there, looked like he was practicing his Roman numerals. The cuts had closed but had not healed, seams designed to be pulled apart for easy access. They were the crisscrossed evidence of man cutting deep and more than once, fully intending to make sure that it stuck. Plip pulled the wristband back and didn't laugh.

Nobody did.

"It's not so uncommon, suicide. Especially here. Well... I'm sure you of all people understand."

"What do you mean?"

Plip shook Ampersand's question away, nodded to the front of the Engine.

Up ahead, Teddy was digging that same knife into the stomach of the gull. There was an unzipping sound as he brought it down, sounded like a man opening a sleeping bag. Placing the knife in his teeth, he reached inside the gull, went elbow deep, pulled out handfuls of pink and burgundy, organs and giblets, threw them to the ground.

"Mind your step," Plip said as Ampersand stepped over a kidney.

Teddy rooted around like he was searching for a prize. He bit down on his tongue and dug deeper, under the rib cage, twisting, threading, pulling. Finally, with some effort, he ripped out the gull's heart.

"Here!" He held it up for the other runners to see, tearing away the bits of vein and artery. There was an *Oooh* noise from the audience. "Here we have the source of the gull's hunger... its life-giver."

Quickly, Teddy shoved the heart into his mouth, bit off a chunk. His pink cheeks flared as his mouth filled with heart-meat. Blood spilled from his lips as he gorged like it was the first time he'd tasted food in years. Within seconds, he'd eaten the whole thing and was looking to the skies with his bloodied maw, sawing the back of his hand across his chin.

"I hope you're hungry," he said, turning to the runners. "As we lose one of our own, we gain sustenance for further running... to keep the planet moving. Take communion, my friends, and eat deeply. Or fucking don't. Whatever. Fuck."

The runners next to him started to rip and tear at the gull themselves, unpacking the gull from the inside out, ripping out chunks of flesh and passing them down the line. From one runner to the next, the hot stink of new death made its way around the running club. Ampersand's nostrils filled with the heady smell as bits of intestine were handed to him. Quickly, he passed it on, hating the feeling of the raw poultry in his hand, now as red as the shirt around his neck.

He tried to wipe his palms against his shorts but was handed another piece and had nobody to hand it to. Everybody in the club had a piece of gull now. In one movement, they lifted their bits of dead things.

"To the road" Teddy shouted.

"To the road!" they agreed, munching down on the food. Some lifted their chins and gobbled down their food without chewing. Some ripped little pieces away and mashed it with their mouths open, masticating loudly with back molars. Others simply thumbed it all into their mouths, stuffing it all in as quickly as they could.

Ampersand looked down at his chunk and saw that there was a nipple on his piece. He didn't think gulls had nipples, but this one did. Maybe it wasn't a nipple. Maybe it was something that just looked like a nipple. But it had the circular brown bit and the pointy end bit and as far as nipples went... this one certainly looked like one.

"Erm... anybody want to swap?" Nobody answered. They were too busy shoveling food into their mouths.

"Eat," said Plip, washing his gull down with more bum-bag water. "You'll need it to keep going. Trust me. Heh."

"But it's a nipple–"

"Eat."

Plip placed his hand on Ampersand's, guided the nippled flesh to his mouth. Ampersand put it to his mouth and saw that all eyes were on him. He tried to imagine he was biting in to a Big Mac but couldn't on account of the fact that Big Macs don't have nipples. He closed his eyes and pushed it into his unwilling mouth, still managing to keep his running steady. He chewed hard. The nipple popped and bitter fluids exploded in his mouth. He chewed hard and fast and swallowed it all down as quickly as possible, struggled to get it past the throat.

Only when he was done did the eyes look away from him, satisfied.

"Remember," Plip said. "Ralph sacrificed himself for this food."

Still with bits of it in his teeth, Ampersand said, "Thank you very much, Ralph."

"You're very welcome, friend," Plip said, smiling wider than ever. He gave Ampersand a big pat on the back and then handed him the water from his pouch. "You are very bloody welcome."

28.

AS THE GULL meat settled in his gut, the bleached orange skies stirred and the wind picked up and Teddy, looking ahead of them all, mentioned that there was a storm coming and that it could turn out to be a bad one and that fucks... he had none to give. But still, people should prepare for a heavy one.

Ampersand kept his head down, said little to nothing, listened to Chris Tangle read from a running magazine, about how there's no greater satisfaction in life than running a marathon.

As the skies turned grey and a cold wind touched their backs, Plip said how his parents used to tell him stories to help get over the storms, asked if Ampersand would like to hear a story.

Ampersand shrugged, said, "Sure."

"Okay then... maybe a story about Ralph... the man who got himself run over by his own car because he forgot to put the handbrake on. That's actually pretty much the whole story. Or, okay... Heh! What about the story of poor Peter Schmeter... the man who nobody could take seriously? Until he fell out of a plane. Nah... that's a boring one. No... hehe. I know which story to tell." Plip licked his finger and pointed forwards. "How about I tell you the tragic backstory of our leader... Teddy Salted. That's a good one."

"Okay."

"Ready?"

"Sure."

"Set."

"Oh."

"Go."

Ampersand sighed.

Plip began.

29.

The Tragic Backstory of Teddy Salted

AS IT HAPPENED, Teddy was born to two parents—Mr. and Mrs. Salted. Both of them were of the standard two-legged variety. This was to be expected amongst human beings. But not entirely unexpected, in Teddy's family, were three-legged babies.

Sometime *way* back along the bloodline was another three-legged man—Reginald C. Salter. And some time way, *way* before him there was another — Mr. Terrence Salt. And there may well have been another three-legged man further back than that, and another one even further back. Who knows?

Not me.

So...

Terrence Salt was born to a wealthy family of salt importers in the winter of 1903 and reportedly drowned in a swimming accident in 1906. He really shouldn't have been swimming at the age of three, especially not tied up in that cumbersome coal-sack, especially not with his hands and legs bound behind his back. Especially not just after eating lunch.

And Reginald C. Salter was raised on a wine farm in Southern France and was reported to have lived most of his life in a cupboard, only being allowed out to stomp on the grapes at the family winery before the sun rose and after it disappeared. Reggie was a grotesquery, a disgrace to his family; his township was fine with those unique cheesy notes he produced in the Châteauneuf-du-Pape, just as long as they didn't have to see him out in the public.

Reginald lived much longer than Terrence, making it all the way to his sixteenth birthday before he was caught out during daylight hours, peeping in through a young girl's window. Not at the girl, mind you, but at her glorious collection of shoes. He was consequently caught, tried, and shot.

His dying words were, "I peed in the wine."

30.

WHEN TEDDY WAS born, it seemed his life wasn't to be weighed down with the same despair and drownings and shootings of his three-legged great-uncles. His parents, both hard-working Christians, decided to bring up Teddy as if he was just like any other kid.

"There's just more leg for the loving!" Mr. Salted said.

"THINK OF THE SOCKS!" Mrs. Salted cried, lost to an existential fugue every time she considered the sock situation—Do they sell socks in pairs of three? Is it even a pair of socks if there are three!?

Mr. Salted gave Teddy all the pep talks and milk a growing boy could ask for, often treating him to his favourite fruit, a ripe banana, whenever the boy showed resolve or leadership or good Christian qualities, like praying and singing and that. You know... God stuff...

Teddy would have done anything for a banana back then. That boy loved bananas more than anything in the world. You could say that he was bananas about them. Anyway, Teddy would eat them all day if he was allowed to and wouldn't die from a potassium overdose. He didn't just eat the soft flesh, either, but the skin as well, and would go on to lick any and all sticky remnants from his fingertips and lips and chin and feet.

Boy, that kid loved a banana!

"THINK OF THE SOCKS!!!" Mrs. Salted said as she tailor-made her son three-legged trousers and shorts and pants. Even on the days where Teddy was forced to wear a skirt, he didn't mind as long as he had a ripe banana.

And of course, growing up with three legs meant that Teddy got called names, had to cut more toenails than the other kids, and was always the last one tying his shoelaces. He couldn't breakdance, couldn't play hopscotch, couldn't touch his toes. He would get picked last for every sport, which was weird because he wasn't even allowed to play sports. Still, the kids would pick him, just so they could do it last.

None of these were that bad, though, not really. Not compared to the fact that Teddy Salted couldn't even walk.

31.

APPARENTLY, IT TAKES most children around twelve months to learn how to walk and that's with two legs. Doing the math, you'd probably work that to be around six month per leg, and you'd be smart to assume it should've taken Teddy a whole eighteen months to begin his perambulations. But it wasn't six months per leg at all.

No.

It turns out the math didn't quite work like that. Actually, each extra leg added an exponentially longer period of time to the learning and it took Teddy a whole seventy-two months before he could walk without support. Yes. Only when he turned six years old was Teddy able to shift his legs in a way that gave him forward momentum, and it took and extra year on top of that before he could stop himself from falling.

It was a strange thing to witness at the time, and his parents couldn't quite believe their luck, seeing him use his feet like a person might do with crutches – outer, then inner, outer, then inner, etc.

It wasn't efficient but at least it worked and now finally, at seven years old, Teddy could walk, and as he walked into school that morning with a whole bunch of celebratory bananas, he told his friends that *at last* he could join them in their sports games.

"You're it," said one of the two-legged girls as she tapped his shoulder and ran away.

"Teddy's it!" said a two-legged boy as he ran the other way.

All of them, running, sprinting as if born to do so.

It turned out that walking was only part of the problem. He still couldn't run. And given how long it took him to learn to walk, the doctors couldn't tell him how long it would take him to learn how to run. They tried to show him on their calculators, typing in numbers and equations before showing the answer on the screen to Teddy. There was no number, though, just a smoking calculator that couldn't compute. *That's* how long it would take.

So, it seemed Teddy would never run, not unless he lived for hundreds and hundreds and hundreds of years. Which was quite unlikely.

"Do you think you will, Teddy?" said his doctor, lollipop sticking out of his mouth. "Do you think you'll live for hundreds and hundreds and hundreds of years?"

"No, I don't think so," Teddy said. "I don't reckon I'll make it past eighty."

"If that!" his doctor said. "Ah well." He ruffled his hair and put another lollipop in his mouth. "Worth a shot to ask."

32.

IT WAS A hard life for Teddy, coming to terms with the fact that almost 90% of child's games involved running. It seemed he would always be *it* or the *piggy* in the middle or the *seeker* in hide and seek. He would forever be the loser.

And it didn't matter how many three-legged trousers or bananas Mr. and Mrs. Salted gave their son, nothing could pull him out of the deep well of depression he'd tumbled into. He was lost to them at the bottom, too far down to hear their comforting words, all but meaningless echoes.

By the time Teddy turned twelve, he tried to kill himself with a toaster in the bath. He'd seen it on a cartoon played for the jokes and figured it was worth a shot. But real electrical systems don't work like that. The toaster sparked, sure, but the fuse blew and the lights in the house went out and then his parents came in and didn't know what to tell him so they gave him a banana.

He was fifteen when he tried again. This time, he gathered all of the sleeping pills he could from his mother's stashed box of tablets and pills and sweets that she kept in a biscuit tin. He went to his room and ate a banana and took the rest of the pills but the banana and the pills didn't mix well and around the time his vision started to blur, he vomited it all back up into his lap. His parents came home, prayed, and handed him another banana.

33.

A FEW YEARS went by without any more attempts and Teddy settled into his routine, never able to run to catch a bus, never able to run to exercise, never able to run for any reason at all until many years later, now working in a shoe testing company, now driving a special car with two clutch pedals, now with a whole wardrobe full of three-legged pants and trousers and socks, so many socks, somebody finally thought of the socks.

Mr. and Mrs. Salted were happy to see that their son had become something of a standard citizen, was paying his TV License fees and his Council Tax on time and was now buying his own bananas, but they could never see how deeply empty their son was.

Like a back garden without a cat turd, he was not quite believable, not quite real, not quite a human being. Not until he met Sandra, anyway. The blonde-haired girl with the impossibly large smile and the Twitter-blue eyes, forever in her running clothes, the one who said she was a running coach and that she liked a challenge and that Teddy looked like a challenge if ever she saw one.

The first time they met, they passed each other on the roadside: her running, him walking. Their eyes caught and she smiled and said how it was "A nice day for a run."

Teddy responded with an awkward "*Hellohowareyouwhoareyou?*"

She didn't answer, already disappearing over the hill.

The second time they met was at the corner shop, picking up milk and eggs and bread and Teddy's daily selection of bananas. They nodded and said hello and she said she liked his third leg and then got all embarrassed because third leg was sometimes used as a nickname for a penis but Teddy lied and said, "I like my third leg, too," as he shoved an entire banana into his mouth.

"Really?" she said.

"No," he replied, swallowing the banana with a single gulp. "Not really. In all honesty, I *hate* my third leg. It's... the bane of my existence. It's useless and cumbersome and I can't run with it and I wish I could get it chopped off. I'd do it myself if I wasn't so scared of doing it."

Why tell her all this? Her pretty face? The potassium high? Destiny?

I don't know; I'm not Teddy.

And neither are you... so don't worry about it.

She *was* beautiful, though. Maybe that was it? A tendon in her jaw flared with each concentrated thought. Apart from the hair on her head, her body was completely hairless, dolphin smooth, something he'd later learn had something to do with being aerodynamic. Even her eyebrows were missing; in their place were two marker-drawn arches.

"Is it really that bad?"

Teddy nodded, let loose his tongue and unfurled his childhood, no walking, and then walking but no running, and will somebody think of the socks, opening up before her like a flower of history, right there in the corner shop by the milk and the eggs and the man buying a lottery ticket.

When he was done opening up, she took a step back, looked from his left leg, to middle leg, to right, and nodded. "No problem," she said, smiling. "Come out with me tomorrow morning. I'll get you running quicker than you can say... erm... erm... quicker than... hmmn..."

She never did finish that thought.

34.

AMPERSAND WAS STRUGGLING to keep up. With both the running and the story.

The storm that came wasn't like any that Ampersand had seen before. It was an emotional one, angry at first, shouting clouds, indignant undulations, sparking with bursts of lightning and growling with thunder. As angry as the storm was, it grew sad and all of the runners felt it, the grief in the tears rained on them; the salt burned their eyes. They empathised and cried along with it, said they were sorry, and pleaded for forgiveness for something they didn't remember doing. Then the storms grew downright abusive, winds whispering criticisms in their ears.

You're too short...

That joke you told at Christmas in 2011 when everyone laughed... they faked it...

Fatty... Fatty fatty fatty...

Your penis is substandard...

Were your parents pork pies? You look like maybe your parents were pork pies...

Even with the barbs on their self-confidence and the mood swings of the weather, they carried on, even as something in the skies writhed, and the runners who caught sight of the movement above felt pieces of their mind, memory, and imagination dribbling out through nose and anus.

"Stay strong, boys!" Teddy called through the rain. "Or don't! I don't give a fuck!"

The podcast host, Chris Tangle, was still in Ampersand's ear, whispering the words left, right, left, right, over and over.

Ampersand checked his phone. They had passed sixteen miles now and his body was hurting, piano-string twinges in the backs of his legs, nibbles in his chest, lung-scraping coughs, and regular thoughts of stop, please, just stop for a bit, please!

Still running, though, pushing past storms above and within, Ampersand turned to Plip and told him: "Please... go on with your story."

That he did.

35.

The Tragic Backstory of Teddy Salted Cont'd

IT WAS JUST gone 7:30 am and Teddy was at the running track, alone, and sure that he'd been set up. He pictured people ready to jump out from holes in the ground like mole-people, holding TV cameras, pointing, laughing, saying, "Look at the three-legged fool! He thought some hot runner girl was going to meet him!" Then they would shake their pointing fingers at him and make *Ahhhh* noises, capturing his emotional breakdown on camera, ready to upload to the Internet for all to see.

Just as he was about to walk home and hate on the world some more, Sandra turned up with a boombox on her shoulder, volume dialed all the way up, nodding her head, even though there was no music playing. She seemed to realize this. So, she pressed the play button and the boombox exploded with powerful drums, twanging guitars, and inspirational arena rock vocals. You know... montage stuff.

If it was to be a training montage, it was a slow and disappointing one. Nothing exciting about watching a man falling down and rubbing his shins and going, "*Eeesh.*"

Sandra explained to him that he was running all wrong, that by doing the outer legs first and then middle leg, he wasn't going to distribute his weight properly and he was going to fall every time. Instead, he was going to have to learn to run like the fingers of a bored person's hand drumming on a table – right, middle, left, right, middle, left. Once in motion, he could not slow or lose confidence; he would have to lean into it, allow the momentum to take over. It would require total commitment.

"But it's too hard!" Teddy shouted, losing his patience with Sandra for the first time. "It's impossible."

"I eat impossible things for breakfast!" she shouted.

"Like what?"

She thought about it.

“Crayons.”

“You shouldn’t eat crayons.”

“I’ll eat whatever the hell I want to eat!” She slapped him, and as he rubbed his reddening cheek, she sighed. “Listen... if you do run like this, even for just a little way, I will treat you to dinner. Okay? A proper dinner. Just me and you.”

“Like a... date?”

“Maybe.”

With fresh inspiration, Teddy tried to run in this new way — right, middle, left, right, middle, left — and he tried and tried until the sun set and his entire body shivered with aches and his knees were covered in welts and the batteries in the boombox were dead.

He tried over and over to get the legs in the right order, tried to mimic that domino leg movement, but he wasn’t committing himself, didn’t trust the three legs that had disappointed him over the years.

On what was supposed to be his last attempt, he got the legs in the right order, but caught the toes of his right foot on the ground, tripped and rolled onto this back.

Frustration howled through him, squeezing his fists tight, whitening his knuckles. “Fucking run or don’t!?” he screamed. “I just don’t care anymore!”

He climbed to his feet and ran again, shouting, “I don’t give a fuck!”

And it worked.

He moved an entire 50-metres before stopping, almost falling again but caught in Sandra’s waiting arms.

Neither of them spoke. And they didn’t go on their date. They were far too tired for any of that. So, they went back to Teddy’s flat and ordered takeaway Chinese food. They ate and watched bad TV shows, his body humming with exhaustion and her with pride, both of them falling asleep right there on the sofa.

36.

IT DIDN'T TAKE Teddy long before he discovered that in this new running configuration, he was able to run for extremely long distances with ease, able to split the effort equally amongst his three legs. And Sandra was a technical running genius, knowing just the right moment to breathe, and when to angle the feet outwards, or when to drink water, or eat, or not.

She started Teddy on a couple of small runs, just the casual work lunchtime jogs, and even though these *weren't* races, Teddy and Sandra still won. Every single time. Even if nobody else was competing, *they* were, and they would high-five and say "in your face" to the other runners' faces and then go out on dates and he would eat bananas and she would eat crayons and then they would have sex.

They didn't walk down the aisle when they got married; they raced. It was a draw. They gave their vows on treadmills, didn't stop moving even as they leaned in for their kiss, each of them racing to kiss the other one first. It was another draw. And then... of course they consummated the marriage. Teddy won.

It was the proudest moment of Teddy's parents' lives. Not so much for seeing their son run, but for seeing him smile for what seemed to be the first time.

To celebrate their marriage, Teddy and Sandra signed themselves up for the Second Heart Half-Marathon. It was to be the biggest run of their lives. There would be TV crews and reporters and lucrative sponsorship opportunities. If they ran well in this race, they could go full time, could end up running for their lives. Plus, this year the event was being sponsored by the *Del Bonky Banana Company* so there would be free bananas for every runner.

How is this not my destiny? Teddy asked himself, barely able to sleep the night before, too busy chuckling with excitement.

37.

"YOU'RE A SHINY golden god."

"You're a blisteringly hot sun."

On the morning of the race, they stared into each other's eyes, whispered affirmations.

"You make me want to explode, you're so perfect."

"I pray at your feet for some of your brilliance."

"You *are* brilliance."

"I am not quite as brilliant as you, because you're *too* brilliant."

"I am only brilliant because of your shiny golden example of brilliance."

"You are the roadmap to my future... maybe if I follow it... I can be brilliant to."

"You're sexy."

"You're sexy."

That kind of thing.

An hour before the race began, more and more of the country's biggest runners arrived. Gary Kane, Thomas Windpipe, Susan Susan, Karen Sandwich, Pat Shandy, and last year's winner—Mo' Tuesday.

Rumour had it, Mo' Tuesday had twenty toes, which gave him an unprecedented balance, unheard of in the world of sports entertainment. Some say he was born that way; others say he had the extra toes surgically added for the advantage. Either way, with his frizzy afro and shovel-wide feet, he was a running superstar and the one to beat.

At 11 am, the starting pistol fired and one-hundred-and-thirty-five runners set off, charging forth like Viking battle maidens, howling for blood and singing for their spot in Valhalla. At first, Sandra and Teddy got lost in the mix of runners but were quickly able to get near to the front, just behind Mo' Tuesday and just ahead of Karen Sandwich, and although they didn't plan it, they were matching each other's pace perfectly. They didn't smile at one another, didn't look at one another, were focused only on the task at hand.

It was a long and difficult run and Gary Kane and Thomas Windpipe overtook them but tripped on one another's shoelaces, knocking them out of the race. Susan Susan lost her footing at mile six and twisted her sense of self-confidence. As such, she had to be stretchered off.

Pat Shandy's legs gave up on him. "Oh, come on!" he said to his legs but they weren't having any of it. He was also stretchered off.

Teddy and Sandra paid no attention; simply kept side-by-side, focusing on their steps and their breathing. Always in with the inhale and out with the exhale.

All was going to plan. They had been riding behind Mo' Tuesday's slipstream and when the time was right, they simply had to flank him, slingshot around him and force him back.

So... something you have to understand is that at the end of every race, there is something called a finishers funnel. It usually consists of two fences bordering the road. As a person enters the funnel, the fences angle inwards, pushing runners closer and closer together, the idea being to squeeze them down into a single file queue as they reach the finish line. That way no two people can finish at the same time. There was only one gold medal to hand out, after all.

The funnel is usually where the screaming fans and the photographers liked to stand. They get to see their sweaty favourites limp over the finish line, get to call out their final encouragements to those about to step over the edge.

Sometimes, when a big company sponsors the event, they like to hand out free samples to all of the runners as a way of promoting the brand. Sometimes, they bring enough for the spectators, too.

The sponsors of this year's run, *Del Bonky's Banana Company*, had brought with them several tons' worth of burlap sacks full to the brim with ripe bananas, practically bubbling over.

The representatives of *Del Bonky's Banana Company*, including Banana-Dan (a man called Daniel who dressed like a banana), had been handing out bananas like nobody's business (well it was *their* business) and at some point, one of the spectators had the bright idea of throwing the exhausted runners a banana as they entered the finishers funnel. It was to be an act of celebration. It was meant to bring joy to the hungry runners' faces.

The problem was that it become a very tight race and there were at least thirty runners gunning for win, all of them pounding into the finishers funnel with nothing on their minds but victory, all of them fighting to claim an inch on their competitors. Teddy and Sandra amongst them.

What the runners expected was a clear and free road, some light cheering, and a man with a stopwatch. What they didn't expect was a road absolutely littered with bananas.

"Here you go, you glorious man! Take a banana!"

"You deserve it!"

"Get this in yer mouth!"

Most of the runners were able to avoid the bananas but not Teddy. His middle foot had always been the slowest of his legs, and he landed squarely on the fruit that had brought him so much comfort in the world. He skidded a couple of meters, rolled, crashed, explosions of hot road on skin. He didn't mean to grab Sandra on the way down, but his natural reaction when falling was to latch on to whatever he could, and when he caught the back of her shirt, she tumbled, and slipped on a banana of her own.

They were the first to go, creating a chain reaction of skidding, legs flying upwards, laces whipping, arms grabbing, bananas in faces, some tripping over the runners next to them. The end result was devastating and it was all caught on camera, broadcasted to the world, uploaded to YouTube, videos to be titled: *Three-Legger Ruins Race.*

A second wave arrived and they ran straight into the fallen, trampling them in the process, splitting skin and breaking bones, crushing fingers and dislocating jaws, smashing heads and popping eyeballs.

Mo' Tuesday won the race. He barely noticed the bananas or people under his massive twenty-toed feet, didn't miss a step as he ploughed right through to victory. A win that would land him sponsorship deals, TV interviews, sports personality of the year, a free pair of toenail clippers, and a furthering lucrative career in TV sports journalism. Mo' raised his arms victorious, unaware of the chaos he'd escaped, took a bite out of his victory banana.

Nobody cheered.

The audience had been silenced, unable to take in what they'd just seen. There was a din of groans and pained cries as the fallen runners started to climb to their feet.

Teddy tried to help Sandra to her feet but she refused it, slapped away his hand, and screamed at him: "This is all your fucking fault! You and your stupid fucked up third leg! You fucking tripod goofy motherfucker! God, to think... a stupid tripod goofy motherfucker just cost me this race because of his stupid tripod goofy, third-legged, motherfu—"

She was trying to stand up as she was shouting at him, her words beating him worse than the fall.

He tried to say sorry, but couldn't get it out before the third wave of runners arrived. Her tirade was snatched from her as a foot landed squarely on her back. A second foot landed on her face and smushed her into the pavement like a baked bean under a spoon. The feet kept coming, looked like they were wiping the concrete clean with her face.

Teddy watched in horror as more runners came. They didn't mean to trample his wife. He couldn't blame them. He barely had time to recognize what was happening before he looked up to see Karen Sandwich bowl right into him. And then more runners, the final wave, engulfing them like they were the last sandcastle on the beach.

They were buried in a grave of bananas and runners and some flyers advertising the local gym.

They died, of course.

38.

THEY SAY IT changes when the sun goes down, and it does.

It gets darker.

The streetlights were just waking up when Teddy stood. Nervous, scared, and quite unsure of himself, he looked around to see that most of the other runners had gotten up and left already. There were bloodied marks on the road, some skin, other dead people sleeping with open eyes, some leftover bananas. Teddy didn't want one anymore. In fact, he wasn't sure if he was ever going to eat a banana again.

He fished through the bodies, searching desperately for his wife, and found her, face down on the floor. He couldn't see where the floor ended and her face began, only the puddle of blood. Shaking now, he moved his hand toward her, daring himself to lift her up, to turn her over and to see.

She would hate him. He knew that. She would blame him for ruining the race and destroying her face.

"Sandra?" he said, voice coming out like a gas-leak. "You okay, hon?"

She groaned and he jumped in his skin (which was quite loose now). Her hands began to move around her and she pressed her palms to the ground, trying to unstick her face.

Teddy backed away. He looked behind him, at the long road away from all of this, and then back to his wife, who was still groaning, still stuck.

"Shit shit shit," he said, drumming his fingers on his chest.

How could he face her, now? How could he look at her?

She groaned again but this time it sounded a little like, "Teddy?" and before he knew it the movement in his fingers moved to his legs and he was running away, faster, faster, into the new opening in side of the road, into the gap.

Behind him, he heard her finally loosen her face from the pavement, heard her voice calling for him but he'd already decided that he would never stop running, not ever again.

39.

IN THE STORM, Ampersand looked at Plip, who had just finished his story.

"Fucking hell," Ampersand said. "His favourite fruit is banana?"

Plip nodded, said, "*Was*... his favourite fruit *was* banana."

PART FOUR

CRACK ON, THEN

"Time flies like an arrow; fruit flies like a banana."
— unknown

40.

THE LIMP FATHER was getting a move on, now, then, always, sweat pearling on his forehead, evaporating as his steps left smoking footprints in his wake, bones grinding like concrete pillars with ancient momentum, breathing in tides, moving moons, rolling oceans.

With his nose to the air and a grin growing on his mouth, he smelled them... the runners. They were on his road, and so he continued to whistle, but harder now. His twee notes like the flap of butterfly wings, little to nothing at first but kicking the air into greater and greater motion. At the end of the road, there would be hurricanes and dead things and people would cry and would accept and would make amends; the runners, would feel it.

Oh, they *would* feel it.

41.

AND THEY DID.

Much further along, the Red Engine Running Society did their best to weather the growing storms, bracing themselves against each gust of wind like waves against the hull of a ship, forcing their feet onwards, sailing the thunderstorm roads, following their leader, Teddy Salted—their favourite lost boy.

"Ha! This is the worst I've seen it!" laughed Plip, the wind violently tousling his hair.

Another runner, a short man with a bullet hole in the back of his head, wearing a crown of skull shards, suggested they had gone the wrong way, said they had missed a turning somewhere, or maybe they should stop and ask for directions, but there had been no forks in the road, no crossroads, and nobody to take directions from. There had been only the way forward and so they called him an idiot and told him to wind his neck in.

Another of the runners, one with swollen eyes and lips like broken thumbs, suggested they turn back. "There's nothing for us this way!" he said, though with his swollen tongue and lips it sounded more like "*Derth's buffing for uff biff... ay!*"

They pretended they didn't understand him. He tried to say it a few times more but they looked at him blankly until he gave up.

"Look," Teddy called from the front. "We can't stop running... we *can't*. If we did then the world would end... or even... the end would catch up with us."

"Too right! Ha!"

"I don't like the sound of that!"

When the storm did calm, it was only for a moment; it simply took an inwards breath, short and sharp before exhaling with double the force. The raindrops as big as apples; the cold winds leaving teeth-marks on the runners' faces and the exposed parts of their legs and arms.

Some runners cried, remembering times past and loved ones lost. Plip laughed about when he used to play in the rain with his brothers and jump up and down in puddles and how he couldn't quite remember what they looked like anymore.

"How long *has* it been?" he chuckled.

Others amongst them sang tuneless ditties. Some sang Madonna hits and a couple of Elton John numbers. Not the later ballad stuff but the rocking earlier stuff, *Crocodile Rock* and *Bennie and the Jets* and that. It seemed anything to keep the spirits up and the rhythms moving.

Chris Tangle offered little to no support through the headphones, appeared to be playing games on his PlayStation, sounded like he'd ordered a pizza. A doorbell and then the hissing *pop* of a beer-can opening and the smell of pepperoni seeping out from Ampersand's ears. His belly rumbled.

"Yeah, you got this, Sandy," Chris appeared to be saying between mouthfuls of beer and pizza. "You just keep running okay? That's the ticket. That's the ticket."

42.

WHEN THE RAINS stopped again, their clothes were sopping wet, their feet opening up with sores and blisters and their fingers numbing, bones shaking in dissolving skin.

"Listen up! I know this is hard and rough but we have to keep going. I'm not prepared to stop. I can't stop. Ever!"

"Why!?" Ampersand called out, his guts in knots, salivating at the pizza-smell.

Teddy looked at Ampersand like he'd bitten his balls.

"Because the world will stop!"

Warmth came to Ampersand's cheeks. A bubble of anger worked its way up through the intestines towards the back of his throat. "How... how do you even fucking know that!?"

The other runners were looking at Ampersand like he'd bitten *all* of their balls, but Ampersand couldn't stop himself now. If he was a ball-biter, then so be it. Desperate rage buzzed through his spine, boiled the blackened blood in his brain.

"Well!? Go on! How the fuck do you know that the world will stop moving!? How does that even work? You can't just go fucking running forever because you don't know what else to fucking do!"

"Hehe... easy now, friend." Plip's hand went to Ampersand's shoulder, but he batted it away.

"Go on... Captain Special-Pants! Tell me why it is that we're running? Because you may have gotten these dead idiots to run for you... following you to the never-ends of the world... on words and lies alone, but not me!"

"My men aren't fools—"

"It's fucking raining!" Ampersand screamed, as if that was all they needed to know.

Just then, the air started to smell like motor-oil, the skies growing humid and muggy, filled with dusty yellow clouds that ran thick with tentacles, noodling purposely through the air, high above the clouds, passing overhead. Ampersand hadn't noticed the tentacles, hadn't noticed that nobody else was speaking, just keeping themselves low and quiet, looking between each other, to the skies, to the shouting man.

"You have to shut up," said Teddy, eyes glaring. "Or don't... I don't give a fuck."

"Yes, you do! Yes, you *do* give a fuck! You're lying to yourself just as much as you are to these people."

Bubbles of blood and snot and pus popped on the end of Ampersand's nose, ran into his mouth, sweet and salty without the popcorn.

"I'm tired!" he said, voice breaking. "I'm so tired."

Plip smiled at him sweetly.

"Come on, chap, hehe. We can talk about this later."

Ampersand couldn't let it go, though. His pace was slowing to a walk, and as such, the pace of the Engine slowed. In his ear, he heard Chris Tangle smoking, choking, crying.

"I'm a failure," the running coach mewled. "Couldn't even get a man to run a marathon on his first go... failure!"

"My feet are killing me," Ampersand continued. "I just want to sit down for a moment... and I want a cup of tea... I don't want to run anymore. I'm..."

The rest of the runners continued, but slowly, holding their breaths, some chattering nervously, others cupping their hands over their mouths and noses, and the one they called Dec exploded with a diseased fit of coughs, hiccupping up a cloud of gnats.

"Pardon me," Dec said, covering his mouth.

How long had he been running with broken lungs? Ampersand wondered. *Are* my *lungs broken? Is my body decomposing out here on the road? When will it be too late to go back to life? Am I dead or dying? Am I rotting or just slow to accept?*

Am I done?

His legs stopped moving.

The engine sputtered to a halt.

"I think I'm done," he said.

The first tentacle calmly broke through the cloud-ceiling, sniffed the air. More tentacles pierced the skies, wended towards the runners.

Dec took out the bugle from his pouch, wiped his dirty teeth, and sounded the alarm before erupting with coughs and flies, but the engine couldn't move, not if Ampersand didn't.

"Come on!" a red runner called to him. "You're letting everybody down."

Teddy huffed, pushed his way through and grabbed Ampersand's head, cupping him like a cute little doggo.

"Look! Look up!"

Ampersand did, slowly, saw the bruised prehensile strings coiling through the air.

"What is... it?" Ampersand said.

"It's the Crack-On," Teddy said, beard hairs tickling Ampersand's chin.

"The Kraken?"

"No. It's the bloody Crack-On. We have to go... and we have to go now. So, deep breath in. Don't overthink it. Just start moving your feet. You get them feet moving and they'll carry the rest of you. You have to be confident, lean into it, don't let your dumb legs get in the way of your running."

"What?"

"Go!"

Teddy pushed Ampersand forward and now the engine was kicking back into life. Too late, though, as the first tentacle snatched one of the runners from the far right. The man, a former banker who'd jumped into the River Thames and drowned in water and responsibility, didn't even have time to scream before he was zipped up into the skies. A second tentacle came and took another, this time from the far left, politically speaking.

Fear struck Ampersand stupid and he couldn't think of doing anything *but* running.

"Good good... you got it," Teddy said. "Keep running... or don't." He pointed to Plip. "Look after the squirt."

"Aye, sir! Ha!"

The engine picked up some speed again, rumbled along, but the tentacles were many. One swiped at the running society's feet, tripping several at once and lifting them away. A handful lost like nuts greedily snatched from the bar.

The tentacles were leathery on their backs and smooth and translucent on their fronts, peppered with sore-looking suction cups, each of them puckering when they got close to the runners, dripping with saliva as they moved.

Ampersand ducked as a tentacle flew past his head. It stuck a runner's face with its suckers, wrapped and twisted, snapped, and pulled the runner away.

"What do we do!?" Ampersand screamed, looking to the skies to see the snatched runners struggling as they disappeared behind the thick sheet of grey clouds.

"Keep running... it's all we have left!"

Lightning cracked the sky and the darker clouds burst, rain and hail hammering down.

Teddy was near the front, standing on the shoulders of his running companions, knife in hand, batting off sky-tentacles, ordering his men to run faster, faster, always faster. Energy gels were passed along from hand to hand to mouth, sucking, sucking, running.

"Keep going," Plip said to him. "Hahaha we can do this!"

Forks of lighting bisected the skies, opened up the clouds and revealed the eye, giant, a full moon of a thing, pupil dilating, blinking lazily. A little below the eye was what appeared to be the Crack-On's mouth. It was smiling. Not the beak of a giant squid or tunnel of teeth like some Sarlacc pit but the toothless gummy maw of a human baby. Ampersand could just make out the red shirts of the runners as they were shoved into its mouth to be sucked to death and swallowed.

The baby-thing, the Crack-On's eye, locked with Ampersand's, the heat of its gaze burned.

Plip went to wrap an arm around him again but Ampersand batted it away. It came again, stronger, and was sweatier, oilier than he remembered. Much more tentacle-like. Plip's laughter sounded out from somewhere behind him.

"Oopsie-daisy! Ha! Looks like the Crack-On's got you, pal! hehe!"

A hug from a boa constrictor, squishing him like a tube of toothpaste, and then he was off his feet, lifted towards the cold screaming skies.

Lighting flashed again and through the white light, there was a three-legged dude leaping through the air, knife raised high, screaming the words, "I DON'T GIVE A FUCK!!!"

Yes... just like with the gull. It was the man's MO, like a kid who'd learned that the single button on the fighting game did the special move and they just do that over and over again because why not? If it works, it fucking works.

Anyway...

"I DON'T GIVE A FUCK!" the screaming leader screamed screamily.

But Ampersand wasn't scared, because he knew that Teddy gave a fuck. Of course he did. The man genuinely cared. Ampersand didn't flinch when the knife flew past his face, didn't move when Teddy rode the knife down the flesh, opened up a sluice of tentacle-goo over Ampersand's face, wasn't all that surprised when it released him, and felt utterly grateful when they both landed on the waiting hands of the other runners, who quickly put them back on their feet.

Somewhere, Plip laughed. So did Ampersand. He was safe again and he looked for Teddy but the man was already back to fighting off the tentacles, constantly screaming out that he didn't give a fuck, didn't stop fighting, or running.

And neither did the tentacles stop grasping and neither did the road end and Ampersand found himself fighting hard now, to fight away the tentacles and to run as fast as he could, anything to help the Engine survive, to save the world from ever stopping.

If misery loves company then the Engine was an orgy, and Ampersand was just happy that someone cared to include him. They were the same as him, these people, all running from something, lost in their footsteps, staving off some inevitable pain like their lives depended on it; better yet, their deaths.

PART FIVE

BAT MAGIC WOMAN

"I'll show you this ghost has blood in his veins."
— Captain Hook, *Peter Pan*

43.

A FEW MILES went by and the Crack-On grew bored, sunk into the skies like a baby dropped into a bottomless lake, waving goodbye as it slipped away. Soon afterwards, the rains calmed and the skies stilled and the Red Engine Running Society continued on.

Why?

To keep the world moving?

Or, so they say.

One of them was supposed to take over his father's funeral service; his first job was to bury his own father. One of them was scheduled for another six-month stint on an oil rig. Another was due back at the base before being flown out for his third tour of Iraq. Last time, he lost his friend and the thought of going back made his heart burn. One of the others had to go home and tell his husband that he lost his job. He bought a bottle of wine, some flowers, but instead of driving home, he drove off a bridge. One of them had just received an eviction notice. Another, a divorce paper awaiting his signature. One of them had been diagnosed with a degenerative brain disease. Another had been given two years left to live. That wasn't what killed him, though. It was the thought of telling his parents. And one of them had just been told that they were expecting a child.

I'm pregnant, Dottie had said.

I'm going to run a marathon, Ampersand replied.

I'm pregnant, she said.

I'm going to run...

I'm pregnant.

I'm going to run...

I'm going to run away...

I'm pregnant.

Can't hear you... I'm too busy running...

44.

WITH EACH SLOW and steady step, the Limp Father's knees cracked and his back popped. He'd caught up with the roadkill a little while back and they'd welcomed his touch as he rolled them up in the road, squashed them down to dust and lost memories, swept them into his snuff box, slotted them neatly into his jacket pocket. He'd caught up with Ravvy... the man in the self-driving car, too, but at the sight of him, Ravvy had ordered his car to speed up, and the thing had driven away.

It didn't matter.

The Limp Father wasn't in any rush.

He would catch up with them somewhere along the road, now or later, it didn't matter when. There was only the road. Everything else was made up by salesmen in navy suits and brown shoes, promising a way off the road, a retirement from struggle. But, eventually, they would learn that it didn't matter whether they thought they were taking a detour, a path less trodden, or had sold their souls at the crossroads. There were no crossroads, no detours, no paths less trodden, only the road.

On which they would all find themselves rolled up in the history sooner or later or right now or maybe even just a moment ago.

Keep running or don't.

It's as simple as that.

A little sustenance, though, the tax man mused. *I am feeling a tad peckish. Just something to keep the feet moving, to keep the hands turning.* Pursing his lips, he whispered sweet reminders, words sounding a little different to anyone who heard them. They fluttered along the road as white bats, clawing angrily at the air to gain flight, clumsily at first before finding their flow, working their way up the road, mewling insane as they searched for fresh snacks.

45.

"SORRY I HAD to take a quick lunch break there, Sandy." Chris Tangle's voice was getting raspy now, his voice slurring. Between each sentence he'd slurp on his beer can, usually followed by the scratching *click* of a lighter and what sounded like Chris sucking on a bong.

Bubblebubblebubble...

"Did I miss anything?" he said, holding the smoke down in his lungs.

Ampersand didn't answer, only looked around at the Engine, full of holes, missing at least a quarter of its runners, all plucked like ripe berries by the Crack-On.

"Ohhh shit!" Chris Tangle coughed, hacked up a lungful of phlegm and washed it down with some beer. "What happened to all the runner guys? I turn away for, like, twenty seconds and they've disappeared? What happened, Sandy? Did they get *tentacle'd* away by some floating thing with a human baby's face in the sky?"

Ampersand remained quiet.

"Ah... it happens, that. Not very often, mind. But it's been known to happen. Some runners get cramps, some hit a mental wall, and others get whipped away by tentacles into the sky. Can't be helped, I'm afraid. That and chaffing."

Ampersand slowed his breathing, tried to get his words out as best he could.

"You knew about the Crack-On?"

"Nope."

"But you just said..."

"Yeah, yeah, I know what I just said."

"So, what else should we look out for? What other flying birds or octopuses or whatever should we be on alert for?"

"Erm..." The lighter sound again.

Bubblebubblebubblebubble.

With smoke in his lungs, Chris said, "Stitch."

"Stitch?"

"Yeah... it's this cramp you get in your diaphragm. It can be quite painful. A real killer."

"Right."

He exhaled, coughed.

"So, you need any inspiration? Seems like you got it. What are you on? Eighteen miles? Who's counting, am I right? You've not stopped running for ages now."

Chris Tangle turned on the TV again. Ampersand heard the opening theme of *Game of Thrones* and yanked the headphones from his ears. He'd not gotten around to watching the latest season and didn't want any spoilers.

The breeze kicked and the dust tickled his legs; it clung to the sweat on his neck. Flies buzzed past his ears and he swiped them away. They passed by his head, invisible, seemed to be just on the edge of his peripheries no matter where he turned.

A runner in front batted at his ear, shouted for the invisible something to "Fuck off!" but there was nothing there.

More of the runners were doing the same now, chopping and swiping at the nothing circling their heads. Some of the runners spoke, muttering angrily to the absence.

Ampersand's neck tickled. Something caught in his throat. It felt a lot like shame.

A man hissed at nothing, whispered that it wasn't his fault that he lost his job. "I wanted to tell you, Dave... I'm so... so sorry."

Another: "I don't want to take the business! I can't... I'm not smart enough to run a funeral home!"

Another: "I can't go back there. I can't bear another minute of it... I can't..."

Another: "She wouldn't understand."

Another: "But I've wet my bed every night since comin' home, mum... every night!"

And, from Plip: "Please... father... understand. Heh... Please."

Dec put the bugle horn to his lips and cried into it, sputtering weak notes. It was unclear if he was signaling for danger or trying to blow the flies away.

Ampersand put his headphones back in.

"What's happening?" he said.

"Do you *shee* them?" Chris said, talking like he was slipping over the edge of drunken understanding, slurping beer.

"What's happening to them?"

"I don't know, I can't see what's happening... I'm asking you... can you see them?"

"See what?"

"The bats..."

"Bats? What bats!?"

"Look... there."

The skies flared, glaring lights from six points in the sky and Ampersand saw.

46.

THE CRYSTAL REFLECTIONS shuddered and the winged critters were there for all to see, stretching wings as they latched onto the shoulders and necks and dipped their noses into the runners' ears as if to drink. The light flared again, another refracting flash and they were gone, invisible once more.

"What are they?"

"I don't have a clue, Sandy. But if I had to guess… I'd say they were some sort of catalysts for change… hungry reminders…"

Chris burped with confirmation.

Ampersand saw colours, the same he might see if his eyes were closed, his fingers and thumbs rubbing against them. Something buzzed and whined like a detuned radio. Ampersand slapped his hand across his face but the thing paid no mind, the frequency drilling into focus.

"Chris?" Ampersand said, seeing the bat now standing on his shoulder, wearing a polka-dotted skirt, hula-dancing towards his ear. "What do I do?"

He couldn't hear Chris anymore. The bat's screeching had *clicked* into place and all other sound was washed out. No more pounding of feet on concrete, of mouths gasping for air, of runners talking to themselves, of Plip's laughter.

Only Dottie.

"Ampersand?" she said, as if she was surprised to be there herself, her voice brandy-snap brittle. "Ampersand… is that you? I can hear you breathing. Have you taken your asthma inhaler? You sound like hell."

"It's me…"

"You sound like you're running."

"I am."

"You sound like you're ill."

"It's worse than that."

"You sound like you're dead."

"I am."

"Oh... and what about me?"

"I think you're fine."

"No... what about me and our baby, Lucy?"

"Lucy? When did you name her? Is it *even* a her? You only found out that you were pregnant yesterday."

"It's definitely a her. And you won't know anything about her if you keep running like that..."

"But I have to run, Dottie. I have to run so I can breathe again!"

"No," she laughed. "No you don't, silly. Just stop running. Let the old man come. Open up your wallet. You have your bank card, don't you?"

"What?"

"Don't worry about it, Ampersand. Everything will be okay. Everything will happen. It already *has* happened. Don't you remember? No need for anything more now. You are only a speck of sand on the shoreline, naught but dust waiting to be washed away with the rest, paupers and kings alike."

"Paupers!?"

"It's the only way! And I can be there, too. I am there... and so is Lucy. You remember Lucy, don't you?"

And for a moment, he did; his beautiful little Lucy.

"Oh, my sweet Lucy."

"She's asking for her father."

"All grown up now, I imagine?" Ampersand said, getting choked up.

"Finished school already. She starts university tomorrow. You're missing it!"

"Oh God... I've missed so much already. But I only wanted to step out for a quick breather."

"Weren't you supposed to walk her down the aisle? She said you didn't show up."

"I didn't mean to—"

"How could you not show up to your own daughter's wedding!? That's so selfish of you... to be dead like that!"

"No please..."

"I hate you, too."

"It's not my fault I died!"

"Isn't it? Lucy doesn't think so. And your grandchildren aren't too happy about it either."

"I wish I didn't die."

"I died a couple of years ago."

"No... please."

"I was alone and scared and there was nobody there to comfort me or to wash me or to hold my hand or to make me a cup of tea."

"Please."

"I don't think I'll remarry. I never did. Came close once, but... it didn't happen."

"No."

"I died alone in my sleep, watching *EastEnders*."

"Not *EastEnders*!"

"The cat ate my nose."

"That fucking cat! ...what cat?"

"I was lonely. Lonely people have cats."

"That makes sense."

"The neighbours smelled me... rotting in the living room... and then they called somebody."

"Nosy neighbours."

"Somebody had to have a nose."

"True."

"And now Lucy and her grandchildren are mourning me."

"What about me?"

"Who?"

"Me?"

"Ah yes... the one who ran away."

"I didn't run away."

"Yes! The one who ran away from us. We pay him no mind. Easier that way. Maybe he stopped his running... came to his senses... maybe he doesn't... maybe he will tell his younger self not to die. Maybe you could have a word with him?"

"Who?"

"You."

"Have a word with myself?"

"It's easy. Repeat after me."

"Okay."

"Stop running."

"Is that it?"

"Yep."

"But I can't stop running... I have to keep going... I have to catch my breath... I have to live again..."

"That's all poppycock."

"What did you just call me!?"

"It's poppycock! You don't need to do any of the sort. Lucy's asking her daddy to stop. Won't you do it for Lucy?"

"Oh, my sweet Lucy."

"Stop running, lie down on the ground, face down, and somebody will be along shortly to sweep up the mess."

"But I can't..."

"Do it for daddy... do it for the tax man."

"But I can't... what did you just say?"

I'm pregnant. I'm pregnant. I'm pregnant.

She laughed in a voice that wasn't her own and her voice, the real one, pierced through mind and memories, punctured the weak illusion.

"Do it for the tax man," the bat said with Dottie's voice, stood on his shoulder, blinking, looking like he'd been caught naked in the bushes. "Erm... I'm your wife."

47.

THE BAT ON Ampersand's shoulder looked deeply embarrassed. Ampersand only had to shrug for it to nod apologetically, before it jumped off of his shoulder and disappeared into the bleached skies, said, "Just doing my job, mate."

Other runners were slowing and stopping and rubbing their ears, renouncing their resolve, assuming the position on the floor.

"Fine... I'll stop."

"I couldn't be arsed with it anymore anyway."

The engine was falling to pieces, dropping to the ground and pressing their faces to the warm floor, pushing out their arms and making concrete angels.

The light flared again and the rainbow bats were on their shoulders; they were larger now, bodies shuddering as they sapped life and inspiration, ripening up and then some. And the runners were drying out, their skin turning to crumpled paper and flaking and their eyes deflating and their hair rolling into spider-legged curlicues before breaking away. The Engine stopped, dropped, and cooked like turkey dinosaurs.

Plip, who was on his knees, prayed to the floor.

"Dad... I'm sorry that I'm like this... I can't help it... Don't hate me!"

His eyes spasmed with movement behind his closed eyelids like a man deep in REM dream sleep.

"Open your eyes," Ampersand said. "Look at it!"

Plip didn't respond, was too busy sleeping.

Without a second thought, Ampersand slapped Plip across the face. His eyes shot open and he screamed, only settling when his pupils dilated, locking onto Ampersand.

"What's... what's happening... heh?"

"Look!" Ampersand pushed Plip's chin to the right to see the rainbow-bat on his shoulder. The thing cocked its head questionably, squinting its eyes now.

"Oh, hello... ha!" said Plip.

Embarrassed, the bat imploded.

Ahead, twenty or so of their numbers were baked into the road, the bats on their shoulders grown into bubbling crystal tumours, foaming like overflowing bathtubs

Ampersand and Plip went to the ones they could help, the ones who were still dreaming, slapping them awake and forcing them to confront the ridiculous nature of their tormentors. Invisible. Afterthoughts. Critical self-talk. Ludicrous when looked at.

They worked their way through to the front and found Teddy, bogged down by the weights on his shoulders, eyes closed, a grimace of strain on his face.

They slapped him but he didn't open his eyes. The things on his shoulders hissed. There were two of them; a bat in each ear. But they didn't stop slapping him, shouting for him to wake up.

When the light flared again, the creatures appeared to be the size of beach balls. Teddy's normally fluid motion was coming out of sync, a symphony with a few broken strings, detuned and playing to a different composer. The whole thing was crashing now! Teddy was looking less like a man born to run and more a de-winged insect, scuttling with erratic paroxysms.

Plip and Ampersand were at his sides, unsure what to do. Plip slapped him again, hard enough to break skin, and Teddy moaned.

"It's not painful enough," Ampersand said. Quickly then, he unzipped Teddy's pouch and reached in. It was deep, seemingly never-ending. He pushed through the gels and water bottles and spare running shoes and what felt like a rotten banana, was in up to the shoulder before he felt the cold steel in his hands. He pulled out the knife, which he saw now was actually a straight razor.

Opening it out, he placed it against Teddy's hand. He ran it across the fingertip and the wound opened like an eyeless socket. It blinked before gushing with blood.

"Owwwww!" Teddy was awake within the second, finger suddenly in his mouth. "What did you do that for?"

"Look, Captain. On your shoulders."

"What the fuck are you talking about..."

He looked.

Saw.

The fat things on his shoulders deflated, lost more of themselves than what they started with; they withered to their bones in Teddy's glare, shattering like flakes of ice and melting before they touched the ground.

Once up and running again, Teddy didn't say anything, simply took the knife from Ampersand's hand, held it up. In its reflection he saw his Engine.

"My runners," he muttered, pointing now to the fallen and wizened soldiers, desiccating on the pavement. "My poor runners."

Dec, who Ampersand had slapped awake only moments earlier, was now more awake than ever, tried to blow on his horn but only flies came. It was enough for the runners, though. Those left alive, lacking some muscle tissue, looking little more than perambulatory skeletons, caught up to Teddy at the front, building a facsimile of the Engine.

Maybe they could have stopped? Maybe they could have gathered their dead? Maybe maybe maybe. But they didn't. Instead, they left their fallen brothers on the road, watching and saluting as they slipped into the rear-view, pressed on.

48.

THREE MILES FURTHER down the road, the man in the self-driving car caught up to them. The car, with its dilating eyeball, panicked, dotting left, right, left, right, moving with insect-like grace, shunted left and right to avoid the dead things, and rolled up alongside them.

Dec blew on the bugle. Ampersand prepared his nose, saw that something had changed with the car, no longer lazily rolling along the road. There was heat buzzing from its bonnet; flies caked to the mint-green paint. It zipped down the window and the runners recoiled and Ampersand hadn't quite prepared enough.

"Whoever smelt it dealt it," the broken voice called from within. "Hehe... too bad I smelt it."

Nobody answered.

"Welcoming bunch, aren't you?"

Again. No answer.

Seeing Ampersand, the shadow-corpse smiled.

"Ahh, so you joined a cult. Good for you."

"This isn't a cult," Ampersand said, before rejoining the silence of his brothers.

They drove and ran in silence, nothing but footsteps and the electric motor for a moment. Ravvy coughed, hacked up a mouthful of dust and then turned to Ampersand once again.

"Well, it looks like he's finally onto us, friend. I saw him a little ways back and I shit myself all over again. He's catching up. He's *cometh.*"

Ampersand meant to stay quiet, couldn't quite do it.

"Who?" he said.

Ravvy chuckled.

Plip mopped his headband over his head, called over. "I say... smelly man. Hehe... who is it that you saw?"

"It was the end, big lad... the tax man... he comes running up from behind, starts singing or something. I don't know. The thing is...

this guy is wearing socks that go all the way over his knees. Madness. And he's not even wearing decent running shoes. But it's not stopping him. He's coming... I saw him sweep away some of the death back there on the road, got his dustpan and brush out and gathered it all into his front pocket."

"His front pocket!?" cried out the runner with the noose-burned neck.

Ravvy nodded. "Anyways... he was about caught up to my rear end when I had to get the car really fired up. Think it's the first time I pushed it past 10 mph in years."

"I thought you didn't want to go to where you had to go," Ampersand said. "To break up with the girlfriend."

"Yes, well... perspectives change when you see the tax man, friend. To see your own death is to see things a little clearer... y'know? What's a little discomfort compared to the endless nothing?"

Dec whispered to Teddy. "Captain... what do you think?"

Teddy didn't respond, didn't even turn his head.

"All I'm saying is. You don't have long. Not at this speed, anyway, friends. Why you running so slow anyway? Something sap your mojo or sumtin? Yeah, not be long before the tax man catches up to you. Not. Long. At. All."

"But I don't want to pay my tax!" screamed one of the runners. "I'm skint!"

Another nodded. "Me too."

Plip said, "Easy now, gents. Ha. I'm sure we'll outrun him. We always have."

"Not for much longer, friend," said Ravvy. "This man is on a mission. I think he smelled some prime responsibility-dodger." The dead man's eyes glanced at Ampersand. "He'll catch you and make nothing out of you. Me? I'm getting the fuck out of here. If you want a lift... I got plenty of room in my car here."

"No! Hah!" shouted Plip, looking a little flustered now. "We can't lose any more runners!"

"But the tax man," said the runner with the broken jaw, so it sounded more like '*muff the math man*'.

"And I've got air-conditioning," added Ravvy. "And leather seats."

"Leather seats?"

"I got seats in here that are so comfy you'll never want to get up again. Serious. Never again."

The one with noose-burns and the one with the blown skull went to him, peered within.

"Teddy!" cried Plip. "Do something!"

Teddy still didn't turn his head.

The robotic eye atop the car peered down at each of the runners, weighed them up. The first of the runners, the one with noose-burns, climbed inside.

"Wow, it stinks in here."

"Don't worry, friend. I just opened a new air freshener. Give it a moment."

"Oh God... what did I put my hand in?"

"Not sure. Feels good, though. Do it again, maybe?"

"Whoa!"

The runner's legs slipped in and disappeared inside the open car window.

"There we go, friend. Next up!"

The second runner climbed inside, made similarly disgusted sounds as he slipped within.

Ravvy burped.

And then a third runner...

And then a fourth...

And the fifth went, but Ravvy said there was no more room.

"It's okay," said a voice from within the shadows of the car. "I think this is my stop anyway."

It was feminine. Ampersand recognized it.

"Okay, then. Well, I hope we got you to where you needed to go, friend."

From the shadows came a broken face, the skin pushed up to the hairline, beautiful blue eyes sitting in the bleached gore of the skull. The always-grin of the lipless mouth. The chattering teeth, clinking medals, legs smooth as a dolphin's back, sans blowhole, the blue running clothes.

"Nice day for a run," she had said as she'd passed him. She must have gotten into Ravvy's car, must have been in there when Ampersand overtook it.

She slinked out of the car with ease and started running.

The fifth and final runner climbed in.

"Well... we're all booked up here. No vacancies. I wish you the best of luck with your future endeavors and with the tax man. I sure hope he crumbles you into dust nice and quick and painless, like." He sniffed, grunted. "Bye, friends."

The five red runners' faces peered out of the window, each of them wearing masks of tired guilt, waving but barely able to look at their fellow runners in the eyes. Ravvy's electric motor screamed as the engine accelerated and the car snapped and crackled along the road, flying faster and faster, swallowed by the dancing waves on the hot asphalt.

49.

THROUGH ALL OF this, Teddy had not turned around once, simply kept his eyes forward. Only when the skull-faced woman pushed past, tapped their leader on the shoulder, did he turn.

"I'm here now," the woman said. "I'm here for that apology."

50.

TEARS ROLLED OVER his cheeks, trapped in his wiry beard hairs. His eyes were raw, scrubbed and bleached. His fringe lay flat against his forehead, some greys that weren't there before, and tiredness, too. The illusion of strength ripped away; the sight of her revealing the truth of him, that he was lost, and like all lost boys, only wanted to be found.

And she had the fucking face on.

Well... she didn't *have* a face, but she looked proper angry.

It was difficult to see, being that she didn't have skin or cheeks or nothing, but she stared at him like the grim reaper and his face seemed to wither, hair thinning out, skin scrunching slowly into wrinkles, etching half-letters into his forehead and the corners of his eyes.

She was a horror, a ghoul from the grave, a face destroyed in the stampedes of the Second Chance Half-Marathon. Her eyes rolled in her skull, searched him. Her broken fingers reached up, brushed through his beard, becoming wet with Teddy's tears.

"My runner," she said.

"I've..." His breath hitched as he tried to get the words out. "I've been running for ages."

And with that, she softened. Well, again, you couldn't see this being that she had no face, but you could still see the anger fading, more from her posture, I suppose.

"I've chased you for just as long," she said. "But an age can come to an end if you let it."

"Your face—"

"—I'm sorry—"

"—is beautiful."

"Don't."

His hands went to her chin, held her straight. He pushed back the loose skin bunched on her forehead, rolling into her hairline. "Sandra... I'm so tired."

"Boy," she said, threading her arms around his middle, locking fingers, holding him. "Boy..."

Struggling to talk through the tears, Teddy forced himself to say it. "I'm sorry. I'm sorry I tripped you up. I'm sorry I ruined our race... our lives... our marriage."

And here she shook her head, struck dumb. Her voice papery thin, ripping down the middle.

"No... you don't understand. I'm here for an apology, yes. But I chased you for so long because I needed to say that *I* was sorry."

"What?"

"When you tripped me... I got so caught up in it and I lost myself... I was so angry. You just got caught up in my disappointment. I'm *so,* so sorry for shouting at you like that. I can't even bear thinking about it too much. I..."

His lips touched her exposed teeth. Blood and strings of saliva and rot connected beard to face. He kissed again, tugging slightly on her hair, the scalp loose on her skull. Through the holes in her jaw, the other runners saw as her tongue wormed towards his open mouth.

She hitched up his Red Engine t-shirt, pulled it over his shoulders. Carefully, Sandra ran her fingers over his broken and misshapen ribs, pressed her palm to the footprint over his heart.

Teddy opened up his straight razor. He pulled bits of his beard taut as he sliced them away, getting rougher with each new chunk he cut. Nicking his face, the slow blood came. He then opened his mouth and put the razor inside.

"Don't," she said.

"It's okay," he said, mumbled.

He placed the razor back into his mouth and pushed it from in to out, pushing against his weathered skin. His eyes clenched shut. He cried out, pushed until the flesh gave and the razor slipped outwards. His infinity-old blood didn't pour but oozed. It wasn't scarlet red but tar-black, like he'd been hooked up to a dialysis machine full of crude oil.

With shaking fingers, he repeated the procedure with his other cheek.

Now smiling, he pushed the razor into his forehead, drew a line around his face all the way to the split in his cheeks. Once done on both sides, Teddy put the razor away and then gripped his cheeks and pulled.

It was difficult, the flesh set for too long. Sandra helped, though, gripping his top lip with both hands and lifting upwards.

They breathed heavy as they pulled, fingers tightening. They inched closer, closer, the mask beginning to slip... a little more... just a little more... keep pushing... a little... a little... yes... yes... yes...

With an orgasmic release, Teddy's face ripped away, revealing his blackened skull beneath. They bunched up his nose and top lip over his forehead, then rolled it over itself so it wouldn't slip back down, tucked it in nice and tight.

With their truths exposed, they did all they could do. They decided they were going to stop.

51.

SOME WAY BACK, Plip clutched his chest, squeezing tight, fingers between ribs, ripping. He wasn't laughing.

52.

AS THE FARMER sows his seeds only to pick his crop, so too, does the Limp Father. By the time he caught up with the dead runners on the floor, they were as grey as the road. The only colour left was their red t-shirts and their neon shoes.

When he stopped to roll the first one over, the body crumbled like a sculpture of ash, the clothes deflating and the shoes tumbling. He whistled and the other bodies followed, each of them collapsing in turn, people-cities burning to dust; it billowed upwards, gathering and pirouetting, spiraling into a twister of hopes and dreams, concerns and nightmares.

Opening his front pocket, the twister tightened its coil and snaked its way inside.

The Limp Father closed it, patted it, and continued to run, stepping on flat empty red shirts as he went.

53.

"WE'RE STOPPING NOW," said Teddy.

"We've got nothing left to run for," said Sandra.

"We've won the only race that really mattered."

"The race to each other."

"To forgiveness."

"To the end."

Silence amongst the few remaining runners.

"No!" cried out Plip. "You can't leave me for that harlot! She comes swanning in here like a hot piece of something-something and you lose your mind! And your beautiful face!? What did you do to your face!? And the world will end if we stop running! You taught us that! The flies will fall out of the sky! The oceans will freeze in place! There will be no new episodes of the news! There will be nothing new ever again. It will all come to a stop. You told us... you told us..."

"And I believe it will, Plip. The thing is... there's always gonna be runners... like you, me, Dec, the squirt... always..."

"I didn't think you gave a fuck!" Plip bellowed, sounding like a punched walrus.

"I do," Teddy said, going to Plip now and patting him on the forehead. "I give a fuck about you. You know that I do."

"But I love you."

"I know."

Sandra spoke. "Why don't you stop with us?"

Plip wiped his eyes.

"I couldn't... I don't want to be the third wheel."

"Nothing wrong with three," Teddy said, middle leg lifting.

Plip tried to laugh but wheezed, cried.

"Stop with us."

"But the tax man," said Dec.

"He comes for us all, eventually," said Teddy. "No better time than now."

"You wouldn't mind?" Plip said. "Me staying with you."

Sandra shook her head.

Teddy hugged him.

"Now?"

"Now."

And the three of them stopped running.

Moments later, and more red runners stopped, too.

Ampersand didn't.

He turned his head, saw them shrink, melting into the great light behind him. They didn't even say goodbye.

"Not many left now, eh?" said Dec. "No... not at—"

Dec tripped on a stone, rolled, knocked himself unconscious.

Ampersand turned to face the front, couldn't stop running.

"Not many left at all," he said.

54.

AT FIRST, HE appeared as a single black dot on the horizon. As he grew, so did their age, their skin crinkling like papier-mâché, their backs arching, Sandra and Teddy's white skull faces touching, yellowing with dark brown dust-caked lines, and Plip, on his knees, arms wrapped around Teddy's left leg, pressing his lips to it, hair falling out with final chuckles, the tax man's steps getting heavier, heavier, the runners' flesh reducing to old dust, a final chuckle, enough to loosen the lower jaw. It exploded on the floor. A final footstep. The three collapsed into one. They spun, mixed, found their way into the Father's pocket.

The old man didn't miss a step.

PART SIX

THREE MORE MILES

"Three more miles?"
— Only three more fucking miles!

55.

WHAT'S THREE MORE miles? Surely nothing in the grand scheme of things? Three more in a world of millions? Only three!? Fucking three!

Why was it taking so long then? Why was it that every time Ampersand peered down at his running app on his phone, it seemed he'd not travelled at all? The currency of each step decreasing, the cost of them rising.

Just three more miles, he told himself, over and over and over...

Just three more miles...

"And then I can catch my breath."

The breeze passed over the road like a curious hand, kicking up dust and ash in its wake but Ampersand didn't notice. He simply moved his feet, his only purpose, his only function.

He was running, and therefore a runner, someone who ran.

We verb therefore we noun.

So, then, the running man could only ever be a runner?

Just three more miles, though...

The forever miles...

Then no more running... no more anything...

The skies turned a deep membranous red, like the road had led him into the lung of some giant cosmic bastard. He focused only on moving his feet.

Left right left right...

Three more...

The skies were veined with pink and swirled with ashy cotton spirals breathing in time with Ampersand's own in and out. He didn't notice the syncing up of sky and body; he didn't notice that his toes had become drenched in sweat and blood or that his head was growing heavier, drooping down a little more with each step, blood-foam bubbling in his brain, spilling out of his ears.

He laughed, didn't know why.

Left right left...

Weren't there a few other runners behind me, he thought. *Weren't there other people?*

Ampersand couldn't remember anymore. He didn't even notice as the road filled up with letters. Only a few dotted the desert dunes on either side of the road at first, some blowing purposely into the road, come alive and desperate for attention, marked urgent and important and stamped with big red letters that said words like FINAL and PAST DUE with official-looking insignias on them, more and more of them appearing as if from wellsprings forcing their way out through holes in the road, the desert disappearing under a sea of paper.

Thinking only of his unborn baby and his precious *three more miles,* he kicked through the reaching mounds of bills and due payments. He laughed again, found momentary comfort in the simplicity.

He couldn't stop now, because then the world would end, remember?

Three more...

The podcast host, Chris Tangle, was still there but a little further away now, no longer talking directly into his eardrum but speaking out from it, as if using Ampersand's ear for a megaphone. He'd stopped offering Ampersand inspirational advice or reverse psychology and had grown bored, drunk, high, had maybe eaten a few magic mushrooms, had started to sing folk songs that Ampersand had never heard before, perhaps making them up on the spot. They were quiet at first and mostly in tune but with each new verse, Chris got louder, the melody grew strange, dissonant, his voice rupturing open like a sack of spores, singing from somewhere in his breaking throat.

There once was a lad from down the way...
Lost his mind...
Lost his day...
Lost the time that he could smile...
And sing the runner's song...

Ampersand moved his feet, moved his feet, moved his feet. The breathing skies darkened and Ampersand couldn't quite remember why he started running in the first place, only that he *had* to keep running, and could never stop, could never stop the left right left right. This was all he was now... movement... movement... movement...

There once was a lad from back home...
The man who ran away...
Left his empty throne...
To make left right left right left right...
And sing the runner's song...

There was once a lad called Ross...
Who didn't like change...
Lost himself in a sea of it...
On a breaking boat full of holes...
And is singing to be gone...

And then Ross became Ampersand...
And, and, and, always, always, and...
More and more and more of it...
Lost himself to the crushing weight of it,
and...
now...
he is gone...

The sides of the road fell away, leaving only the road as a bridge in darkness, void-black, stole the light from your eyes and offered nothing in return. His footsteps echoed loudly, reverberated up the road and back.

The wind went and left none of itself, no atmosphere at all. It wasn't hot anymore nor cold. It was the point in-between.

An unopened bill, resting precariously on the side of the road, tipped over the edge, tumbled into nothing.

But the darkness eased. Starlight glittered on either side of him, watercolour nebulae, distant galaxies coiling, unfurling, blooming like flowers in sunlight, stars exploding like fireworks, comets flying overhead and drawing lines of white, telling stories and constellation-myth.

As he ran, the growing space around him didn't stop. It expanded. The glistening display of colour and light reached further and further outwards. The glowing sands of space-dust disappeared into the dark, the comet-wakes faded away, and the galaxies uncoiled, shattering slowly, and each piece moving further and further away, little dots of light leaving Ampersand without saying goodbye.

And just like that...

He was in the darkness again...

"Why don't you check your phone?" said Chris, his voice deeper than before, the signal breaking.

Ampersand obliged, lifted his arm with great difficulty and saw that he only had a mile left to go. He also noticed how withered his fingers were, like old twigs wrapped in cling-film.

"A mile, Sandy. That's great work. You've nearly completed your first marathon. How do you feel?"

Ampersand didn't answer.

"Good. Good. Concentration is key now. You don't want to fuck it up at the end, do you?"

Still no answer.

"A little further... and then you can be alive again. I promise."

There was a pain in his side, a twisting in his guts. A stitch.

His echoing footsteps doubled up.

There was a tune. Not from Chris. Not from Ampersand, but from the man behind him—the Tax Man.

He had *cometh.*

56.

"YOU MAY AS well give up now," the voice said from behind him. It was the voice of a grandfather, genteel, the kind of voice that you would sit next to and listen to its stories. Of which he must have a lot to tell. "You're running out of road."

"Don't listen to him, Sandy. Listen to *me*, your coach. Keep running. You're so close now... so close..."

"My sides... hurt."

"I did warn you about stitch. They can be a killer. Don't worry, just keep breathing."

"I'm trying..."

"I know, Sandy. I know."

Up ahead, in the darkness, was light, an opening hand of golden sunlight.

"How..." Ampersand tried to speak, coughed up a mouthful of dust. "How long left?"

Ampersand lifted his phone. His wrist was stick-thin, fingers weak. But he saw it...

One mile left.

Still...

Up ahead, he saw Ravvy's car. It was empty, bathing in the sunlight, by its side were the runners, each holding handfuls of Ravvy — some holding his face, others his heart, others his lungs, skin, etc. They were dead, more than dead, petrified, must have given up at some point, or is that still yet to come?

At some point in the future, everything has already happened, remember.

Ampersand ran after them, lost a toe, felt a lung collapsing, something inside him crumpling like squashed origami.

Still one mile left.

Ampersand ran... and saw that as he ran the light at the end moved further away, the last mile never quite finishing. He'd passed the car, the green paint now speckled with rust, ancient. The bodies collapsed. Behind him the Father sniffed them up, wiped his nose.

Ampersand ran until he was no longer in his own mind. He was his own shadow, flat against the road and dragged along by his physical self. And then, he was no longer the shadow but his left foot, aching and broken, stressed and split, wondering why the thing up top wouldn't stop. Then, he was the smell he left behind. And then, a leftover, unfinished thought. And then, he was the old name, Ross, doomed to be lost in the change. At some point, he was the Limp Father himself, looking at his own back, chasing. The one in front looked over its shoulder and it was him, confused.

"What?" he said.

"What?" he replied.

And then, he was back in his own head again, being chased, chasing that twenty-sixth mile but the road was growing longer and he was getting older.

He ran... in all languages and senses of the word... Ampersand ran.

And, yet, there was still one mile left.

57.

THE LIMP FATHER spoke:

"You think that I am chasing you. I am not. I'm not a character, lad, but a function. You think that you will finish this run and you will be free of it but you will not. There is no end to the race, only more running. I will tell you again because you need to understand... there is no end.... there is no end."

Still one mile left...

Each step only pushed the finish-line further away. The Father was right. There was no end to this. Ampersand slowed to a stop, let his feet find the ground and felt the world beneath him, unmoving.

He closed his eyes, let the warmth of the light fill him up; he drank deeply from it.

I only wanted to catch my breath, Ampersand thought.

He inhaled deeper than he ever had in his life (and death).

When he opened his eyes again, turning, he saw the Limp Father was standing, too, silent. He was smiling at Ampersand like a neighbour peering over a garden fence.

"It was a nice day for a run, wasn't it?" the Limp Father said.

"It was," Ampersand said, smiling.

"Better to accept it, sooner the better."

"I only wanted to run a marathon. I wanted to run a marathon and become alive again."

The Limp Father's grin fell away, leaving only pity and concern.

"I'm sorry, boy... I really am... but that's not how this works."

"But my podcast... Chris?"

Chris was crying, blubbering into his microphone.

"I'm sorry, Sandy."

"But you said..."

"I know what I said. I'm a success coach. This is how it works! I say things, *anything*, to inspire..."

"But you said it would make me alive? You said..."

"I make unattainable promises that inspire people to move. It's not my fault if the promises aren't true, is it?"

"No... no... I guess not."

Ampersand looked at his aged hands, the skin flaking, tumbling from him with each movement.

"I ran to the end of the universe."

"Yes, you did."

"Because I was scared."

"We're all scared."

"It was all changing... too much... all the time..."

"Even your name."

"Exactly."

"Change is one of the few constants."

Ampersand's brain started to bubble, pulsing, pushing against the backs of his eyes and in his ears.

"Is there anything else after this?"

The Father shrugged.

"But I won't get to meet my baby?"

"No."

"Or see my wife grow old?"

"No."

"Or watch the next season of *Stranger Things*?"

"Oh, well, that's... no... no, you won't."

Ampersand dropped to his knees, shook loose some dust. He pressed his face into his hands and cried.

The tears were warm, filling his palms, running through fingers, smelling of pennies stolen from stagnant wishing wells. The bloodied tears poured through his nose, out his ears, spilling from his face, leaking from somewhere within. Thin rivulets spurted from his tear ducts in slim eruptions, slapping loudly against the concrete floor. Thoughts of his unborn baby, his wife, his mum and dad, job, friends, garden fence that he painted, his nice big TV, the donuts from the cafe by the office, dipping his foot into a hot bubble bath, crunching ice cubes between his teeth, flicking spiders, tiny pleasures filled the gaps in his mind where the blood had given way. He remembered brushing his teeth and drinking the mint-cool tap water. He thought about the feel of camping chairs holding his butt, and a perfect cup of tea, like his mum used to make, and cheese sandwiches. He pictured his daughter, or son, wondered who they might grow up to be, what pleasures they'd find, what stumbling blocks he'd help them over. He pictured him and Dottie, old, holding hands, floating over their town, waving to friends, riding fireworks over the hills, exploding with held-hands, hugs, kisses, the ashes of their love raining like nuclear fallout, finding their way to the rivers, and then the estuaries, then the seas.

"I'm not ready yet," he said, spitting chunks of dried gooey blood off the edge of the road.

The Limp Father simply nodded.

"Time waits for no—"

Ampersand took a step forward and the Limp Father took a step back. He took another, and the headphone he'd ripped from his ear lifted up, snaked back into his ear. Another step and it found its way back in. The Limp Father took another step backwards. The man's face was a grimace, confusion. Ampersand walked, tiredness leaving him. He watched as bits of skin floated up, slotted into him like missing jigsaw pieces.

He smiled.

Took one more breath.

And then, he was running again.

And as he did, the Limp Father ran backwards and everything reversed, the stars and moons and comets returned, pulled back together, tight, clenching into smaller and smaller fists.

Faster now.

More blood and bits of brain fell from out of his nose.

Some memories. A familiar smell, now not so familiar.

He ran, body filling up with vitality, pumping arms and legs, breathing, *really* breathing again.

The darkness retreated and the podcast host who was drunk and high started to sober up, his slurred words coming into sharp focus, revitalised by the man running backwards, inspired to become better.

Run.

Run.

Run.

The raggedy clothes on the floor, holes stitched back together, dust piling up, making men from nothing, a working engine from broken parts. They stood, ran with him, backwards. The Limp Father was ahead of them. They couldn't catch up.

From his pocket poured out another man and a woman and another man. Two pulled their faces back on. The three-legged runner in the three-person relationship re-joined them.

The Crack-On placed runners on the road like it was positioning action figures on a playset, putting them back in the race.

The Red Engine Running Society went from nothing to something, before vomiting up the bits of gull and piecing it back together again, letting it fly from their hands like a white dove at a wedding. They waved it off, once scared, this time joyously.

And in return the gull's friends pieced back together their lost runner—Randy—delivered him back to the road like a cherub before circling up and away, cawing their goodbyes.

Faster now... faster... huffing in deep breaths, oxygen filling up the space in his skull where the blood was. Excitement and happy tears and his arms pumping wildly.

"Home!" he declared in reverse. "Emoh!"

Ampersand said goodbye to his friends, running family, and ran past the reversing car, taking its passenger back to the start, perhaps to make different decisions, perhaps to have those awkward conversations and move on to better relationships, or perhaps to retread the same ground. The option was theirs.

Still running, screaming, screaming, arms in the air, the roadkill waving their hands as if celebrating the victory run of their favourite athlete, waved him through, cheering, cheering.

And there... up ahead...

The finishers funnel...

No fences but trees, arcing over into a tunnel...

Blood and brain and memories still bursting from his face, shaking, arms up to the sides, knees up to his chest, Ampersand ducked his head as he entered the tunnel...

"Back to the start!" he screamed, disappearing into darkness, the trees twisting around him, spinning, his brain now completely empty of the blood that drowned it, seeing stars, thinking thoughts, tasting love, hoping for more, heart beating, eyes streaming clear, pulse thumping, heart beating, a baby crying, heart beating, a baby is crying, and a heart is beating. "Back to the start! Yes! Back to the start!"

The Limp Father closes his pocket, pats it shut.

58.

. . . BUT NOT YET.

Don't get me wrong, the Limp Father *will* collect Ampersand. Not only the man but his bloodlines and memories and however many names he acquires throughout his life. The Limp Father will snatch up everybody, everything, but always *eventually*, always at the end and Ampersand wasn't there yet. He'd run to the end but was back to now, putting off escape for tomorrow or maybe even the day after that.

He didn't hear a thing as the gap blinked shut behind him. He slowed his run, simply breathed, felt the morning chill on the backs of his arms, the back of his neck. Peering over his shoulder, he saw that the corner of the police station garages and the corner shop now met, the pebble-dashed walls fixed together as was originally intended.

Ampersand didn't stop. He left that gap and returned to the blue-world he'd left only a moment prior. It was only just now starting to wake. The cinnamon-scented sun peered over the horizon, the shutters of shops rolling upwards, cars now on the road, a man passing by on a bike nodding at him.

"Morning," the cyclist said.

Ampersand simply waved, turning into the end of Downside Drive, running past an elderly lady in a dressing gown wheeling in her bin.

"Hi," Ampersand said.

She didn't reply.

Once back home, he kicked off what remained of his shoes, and walked into the living room, heard the creaking bed of a slowly waking Dottie upstairs.

Ampersand removed the headband and used it to wipe the muck and dirt and dried bits of blood and brain from his face and threw it all into the kitchen bin. He ran the tap cold and poured himself a glass of water. He sipped it, felt its cool running down into his middle and thought maybe he'd never had a more refreshing glass of water in his life.

Filling the kettle, he then placed teabags in two empty mugs, placed two slices of bread in the toaster, stood and looked at the empty wall next to the fridge, felt his bare feet on the linoleum floor.

"Ampersand?" Dottie said, rubbing her eyes as she slowly walked down the stairs.

"Mmn?"

"What are you doing?"

"Nothing," he said, lied. "Relaxing, I think."

She came in, held him from behind, burying her face into his shoulder. There they rocked, swayed gently as the kettle boiled and the toaster popped.

"I'm thinking it would be nice to put some of the kid's drawings and photos and that on this wall."

"We could even measure him against the door frame just there. Once a year. See how quickly he or she grows."

"I think he or she will be great."

"Great at what?"

"It doesn't matter."

"No, it doesn't."

"You smell."

"I know."

They stayed like that, dreaming of all the gifts waiting for them further on down the road, dancing softly and silently, left, right, left right, left right.

Luke Kondor
Sherwood Forest
November 2019

ABOUT THE AUTHOR

LUKE KONDOR started writing on his computer in his early teens and never looked back… and now he has very sore eyes. He also runs and produces a short story podcast called The Other Stories, which has amassed over 8-million downloads and has a monthly listenership of ~200k downloads. He has two novellas coming out in 2021 with small presses Eraserhead Press and Bizarro Pulp Press (this very book). In 2015, he won the best Low-Budget Film Award at the London Short Film Festival for a film he made in 7 days with no camera and no money.

Currently, he works from a dining room table in the middle of Sherwood Forest and lives with his fiancée, Cat, their pet cat, Oscar, and their larger, angrier cat, Alaska, who is actually a dog.

CPSIA information can be obtained
at www.ICGtesting.com
Printed in the USA
BVHW031705030921
615980BV00010B/728

9 781950 305711